Colt O'Brien Grows Up

A Novel

By

George Matthew Cole

Printed in the United States of America

First Printing
ISBN-13: 978-1480051812
ISBN-10: 1480051810

Original cover art by Terry Smith
Cover design by George Matthew Cole

**For more information about the author and his work, please go to
www.georgemcole.com.**

This novel is dedicated to my wife
Kandis Lynn Weiler Cole

She sees beyond this world.

ACKNOWLEDGEMENTS

Thanks to Roberta "Jean" Bryant for assessing my work and providing encouraging input.

A writer's life can be a lonely one. I am fortunate to be a member of two writers groups where I present my unfinished work to a captive audience. Their support and fellowship, throughout the years, has been invaluable.

Sallie Tierney, the author of "High Tide and Low Expectations" has been the leader of the Burien Seniors Writer's Workshop for many years. I consider myself lucky to be a member. She has created an environment for both aspiring and accomplished writers that provides support and constructive criticism. My special thanks for the great work that she performs.

Lastly, thanks to all family, friends and colleagues who have encouraged me. You know who you are.

NOTE FROM GEORGE MATTHEW COLE

After reading "Colt O'Brien Grows Up" please take a little time to write a review and submit it to the bookseller of your choice. Written reviews are important to the author and potential readers, as well. The review can be as little as a few sentences or much longer. It's really up to you. I hope you will enjoy my book but, even if you don't, please write a review.

Thanks George

Colt O'Brien Grows Up

Chapter 1

------Email-------
From: Lathrop, Gerry[GerryLathrop@WWU.edu]
To: O'Brien, Colt[ColtOB@yahoo.com]
Subject: Welcome

Hello Colt
Welcome to Western. I am in charge of our diversified computing network here at Western. I look forward to having you on my team.
We have a mountain of work with very little experience. Your talents will be needed and appreciated. Please come by my office as soon as you get settled in.
I see this as a win/win experience for you and for Western.

P.S. I know your background is with Microsoft operating systems. We have many PCs using Windows as well as a few NT Servers. Also, we have UNIX servers and workstations with a few Apple boxes.

See you soon
Gerry Lathrop

------Email-------

The bright northwest sun radiated onto the Western Washington University campus. Nearby the small city of Bellingham lay nestled in northern Washington just south of the Canadian border. The dark blue Pacific Ocean sparkled and small waves lapped against Bellingham's shores. This September day the campus resembled the PR materials that were sent to prospective parents, students and teachers. The golden brick buildings overlooking languid trees and green grass were the perfect image of an esteemed educational institution of higher learning.

School opened in one week. This was the day for students to move into the dorm buildings. Harried, excited, teenagers and their parents had awakened the campus from the deep sleep of an overcast summer. Beneath the brightly shining sun, the air was thick with anticipation. Only the "out of state" newcomers took this sunny day for granted. Locals felt like a little bit of paradise had been given to them after the rather cool and cloudy recent months.

Three freshman teenagers stood gazing at the gushing fountain in the center of the campus. The bright sun beat down forming miniature rainbows in the mist. All three seemed to be surrounded by an aura of optimism and connected by the bond of friendship.

The girl stood at five feet seven inches tall with a trim athletic body. She wore aqua Bermuda shorts and a light green blouse. Her light brown hair was pulled back into a ponytail revealing an oval face of clear, lightly tanned, complexion, but little makeup. Amy Strong's emotional world reverberated with realized and potential happiness. She glowed outwardly and within. Her thoughts projected a coming year of continued success on the soccer field and in the classroom. She relished the challenges that faced her. But, her most precious thoughts were of the young man who stood by her side. Being with him gave everything a deep satisfaction. Going through the coming months together would be a dream come true.

Colt O'Brien at just under six feet, was the shorter of the two young men. He projected a sense of coiled energy behind a calm exterior. Dark black hair framed his intense deep blue eyes. He wore a pink T-shirt with gray denim shorts. His old-style sneakers were black. Colt foresaw achievement and success ahead of him. He pictured himself as a brave warrior attacking technical computer problems. For him, freshman year could not start soon enough. Schoolwork was important, but most of all Colt craved respect in his field of endeavor. Being anything but the best computer technologist was unacceptable. His job as a system administrator for the university network would give him the chance to prove himself. He envisioned Amy by his side, looking at him with pride and loving admiration.

The bright blue eyes of the taller student, Bobby Jones, danced with excitement, while following the movement of the gushing water. Unlike his best friend, he appeared to be relaxed and available for life to come at him as it may. He wore a white T-shirt with shiny blue sweat pants and sandals. He thought of the happiness of his boyhood friend and hoped that he would be as happy some day. After seeing so many girls on campus earlier, it was difficult for him to focus on anything else. It was like he had been sleeping in a world where the female half of humanity did not exist; at least not as sources of sexual attraction. Now he was wide awake with pretty girls everywhere. He was caught staring more than once by friendly co-eds, some of whom stared back.

It was late afternoon. The work was over and everyone involved was relieved. Because of the lack of parking and easy access, it had been a trying task to move the students into their new homes. The maneuvering of vehicles into position that were loaded with an assortment of furniture, computers and other belongings, caused backups and delays. With the anxious freshman students it had been especially trying. Earnest parents, siblings and friends had helped with the work that finally was finished. Now, the helpers were headed south toward Seattle on Interstate 5 and to other parts of the state on other highways.

The sun shone like this rarely, in Bellingham, Washington. When it did, all residents felt rejuvenated. It was like emerging from a cave after a long hibernation. Even though it had been sunny for the past few days, the novelty had not worn off. Gray, rain filled skies could be upon them at any time.

Colt O'Brien thought about his journey to this spot on this college campus. He turned to his friend and smiled.

"Bobinator, I guess you never thought I'd be standing here at Western. Man, I was ready to just work and skip the whole college thing."

"Yeah, nobody thought you would be here. You can thank the geeky kids in the Microsoft cert program. Hell, without that certification you might be fixing PCs making ten bucks an hour. No way you would be living at home, either," said Bobby Jones.

"Hey, my old man would be really pissed if I wasn't here. My mom would stick up for me no matter what, but it would be a pain. I guess I was into my own space then and needed a kick in the ass. Now that I'm here, I plan to do something great," said Colt with a confident smile.

"You sure got noticed with all the stuff that happened last year."

"I found out that there is more to getting an education than I knew about. Crap, I'm surprised that I made it through all that. But, all that studying paid off. And, I know how to do it now," boasted Colt.

As Bobby and Colt continued talking, Amy Strong, stared into the fountain as if it were a crystal ball divining the future. She smiled and her eyes began to glisten.

"Dude, when school starts next week, I plan on attacking my classes like I did that cert test. And, I'm not beat up now like I was then," said Colt

"Man, I wish I had someone like Amy to help with studying. Doing it alone is a drag," moaned Bobby.

Colt's inner senses became attuned to his friend at the mention of Amy. In all the years of their friendship, Bobby had never demonstrated an interest in the opposite sex. The fact that he was an honor student also was an obvious tip off that something was different now.

"Well, Amy sure helped me but I don't remember you needing any help," kidded Colt.

Bobby's face reddened a bit as he nervously looked to the sky.

"I guess I just might like to have a girl to study with," he said sheepishly.

Colt grinned at his friend and winked.

They both turned to Amy and were taken by surprise to see her light, blue eyes filled with tears. Colt put his hand on her shoulder.

"Are you okay?" asked Colt.

Amy turned and hugged Colt while continuing to sob softly.

"I'm so happy we're here together. I have never been this happy."

Colt smiled with relief when he realized that the tears were of the happy variety.

"I am too, I am too," he said.

Chapter 2

------Email-------
From: O'Brien, Colt[ColtOB@yahoo.com]
To: O'Brien, Kelly[Kellyobrien@UW.edu]
Subject: What a year

Hey Sis
Man, I can't believe the senior year I just had. It was scary and cool at the same time. Even I wonder how I made it through. And, I never think back and worry about stuff. I bet Mom and Dad can't believe I'm in college. You can tell me what the first year will be like so I don't screw it up. Stay tuned for more big stuff. I know this year will be rad.

Later
Colt

------Email-------

After returning home to Normandy Park for the week before school started, Colt tried to relax and conserve his energy for the year ahead. He met with Amy a few times but for the most part kept to himself. A common day consisted of sleeping late, and walking along the beach or on trails. In the evening time was spent on the computer or watching television. He knew that his life would soon be full of books and reading. He avoided both.

Colt felt relaxed, comfortable, like being at a vacation cottage on the Washington coast. Everything was familiar but foreign at the same time. Vivid colors grabbed his attention. *I can't tell if I have legs or not. I must be in a dream.* He allowed his mind to settle into a non-active state. becoming still and receptive.

6

Colt had a special relationship with dreams. For Colt dreaming was like living in another home. It was a familiar world. Almost always, there was a hidden message within his sleeping visions. Although the messages were usually obscure, most of the time they foretold future events. He had come to see his dreams as prophetic, but usually didn't understand their meaning until something happened. He wanted to use his dreams to help him deal with things, but in the past had been unsuccessful.

From within his detached state of mind, Colt recognized what he was seeing. It was as if he had pushed a replay switch and was reliving the past. *Hmmm…this is different. I don't usually see the past.* Each scene emerged, was absorbed and then was replaced by another. A delicate rhythm developed within the mind of the sleeping young man as the images flickered across his inner vision.

In one scene Colt was looking at a computer screen with an exam question displayed. There were multiple, lengthy answers beneath. He instinctively knew which was correct. A strong sense of accomplishment and elation came to him. The next scene was one of a sun behind a blanket of fog. Colt could feel and see the light behind the gray-white haze. It was like an enormous magnet pulling him forward. As in so many dreams before, he could not break through to the other side. He felt stifled and inept.

After turning away from the impassable wall, the moving panorama of colorful images continued. They were scenes from his recent past. Each one reminded him of an event. When he saw the image of a thirty-something woman with dark hair, he recognized her as Alison Monroe. Pangs of fear disrupted his tranquil state causing him to flee. *Ahhh! I have to get away!* He tried to run but began to spin in dizzying circles. *Oh, oh, now I remember. It's only a dream.* Then, Colt woke with a start. He still saw the face of Alison Monroe staring at him with lifeless eyes. A shiver ran from his feet to the hairs on his head.

Colt lifted his head and sat up in bed. His dark, blue eyes still reflected dreaminess beneath his full head of tousled black hair. He remembered he was in his bedroom in his home in Normandy Park, Washington. It was late morning and the sun was shining through his bedroom window facing the Puget Sound. After forcing the negative vision of Ali Monroe from his mind, Colt resurrected the uplifting images from his dream. As he mulled over fond memories of achievement and overcoming adversity, he was interrupted by a knock on the door.

"Colt, are you awake?" chimed a singsong voice.

"Yeah, Mom. I just woke up. I had a long dream," answered Colt.

"Come in the kitchen. I'll make you something," she said.

After a few minutes of lying in bed, Colt jumped up. The aroma of fresh coffee and bacon floated throughout the house. He hurried to shower and dress. After sitting down at the kitchen table he looked at his mother Leona. She was petite with blond hair and green eyes. Worry wrinkles around her eyes were noticeable. *Uh oh. She's worried about me,* thought Colt.

"Honey, I hope you didn't dream about the future. I worry about you using your special abilities to see and know things. I know how powerful it can be but I think it's dangerous too.

Colt thought about the fact that most of what he had dreamed was from the past. *I wonder if I'll stop having psychic dreams. I hope not. They're sorta fun.*

"Don't worry about me. Most of my dream was really good. And none of it was about the future," said Colt.

"Tell me about the good parts. I am going to miss you so much when you go away college," she said.

Colt thought about his mother. She was his biggest supporter and knew about his special abilities. But she also worried a lot.

"Oh, I just dreamed about the stuff that happened last year. Man, a lot happened didn't it?" smiled Colt.

"We are so proud and happy for you. You set a goal and got that computer certification. You have a wonderful girlfriend. And, you're going to college. Isn't it wonderful?" she gushed.

A vision of Amy came to him. He could see her slim athletic body, brown hair and bright blue eyes. He felt a wave of happiness wash over him causing goose bumps to form.

"I guess I'm pretty lucky. I got a lot of help from a lot of people," said Colt.

"Yes, many wonderful people were supporting you. And your father seems to be very proud of you, too."

"Well, it's not perfect but the thing with Dad is a lot better," said Colt.

"Your father loves you. He just has a hard time showing it. I think you going to college made him very proud."

"Hey, it's better with him than it has been in a long time," answered Colt.

Tears started to form in Leona's sad eyes. She did not try to stem the flow.

"Oh honey, you'll be gone in a few days. My baby boy won't be in the house. I can't help it. I miss you already."

Colt jumped up and hugged his sobbing mother.

"Don't cry Mom. I'll still love you just as much as ever. Maybe more."

"I know honey, I know."

Colt remembered how close he came to not going to college at all. It was falling in love with Amy that changed his attitude toward school. She was the reason he pushed himself, after cruising through most of his high school years. As if by fate, opportunities were presented to him along with support from many people. Changing his life was challenging but the desire to succeed fueled his efforts. When he passed the Microsoft Certification Exam everything fell into place. *Man, I didn't think I would get through that test. I was almost dead. Then I saw that blazing light. No way I'll ever be the same.*

Just as Colt was sitting down at the kitchen table to eat, his sister Kelly walked into the kitchen. She smiled brightly and kissed Colt. Her blond hair shimmered.

"Well little bro, are you ready for the big university up north?" she asked.

"Yeah, I'm ready. Got any tips for me?"

"Don't get too cocky. From what I heard, you will have way more stuff to do than is reasonable. It took me awhile to adjust when I got there. Between soccer and studying, it was like I never had a minute to myself."

"Yeah, I guess it's a big change. I'll try to be more humble," said Colt.

Kelly pushed her brother's shoulder and laughed.

"Good luck with that Bro."

~~~

A day later the weather had changed showing hints of fall. Amy sat on a bench at Seahurst Beach Park. She stared at the Puget Sound as raindrops splattered the water's surface. The dark, overcast, wet day reflected her mood. Although the future should have been filled with great possibilities, she had an empty feeling. She thought about her success in the classroom and on the soccer field knowing that she should be enthused about attending college and being a member of the soccer team. *I should be more excited about going to college. But, I'm having a hard time caring. I just want to get it over with so Colt and I can be together. What's happening to me?* A wave of anger rose up in her, as she threw a rock into the water. *I'm not supposed to be like this. It's college first and then the rest of my life. I guess I'll just keep telling myself that. I wonder if it will work.* Amy knew that following the plan would end up in success. She had followed the plan all of her life. But now, the plan loomed in front of her like a wall of giant boulders that were sitting between her and the love of her life. *Oh well, I'm sure it will all work out. How bad can it be?*

Chapter 3

------Email-------
From: Lathrop, Gerry[GerryLathrop@WWU.edu]
To: Joyman, Bill, Bill[JoymanB@UCBerkeley.edu]
Subject: Windows is crap

Hey Joyman
Just be happy you aren't up here in Windows land. I am
so sick of people acting like Microsoft is worth a shit
and Windows is a real operating system. And I have to
support it. I feel like quitting and being in a UNIX only
shop.
Later
Gerry

------Email-------

Gerry Lathrop was starting to simmer like a tea kettle just
about to boil. He was large and round with rosy cheeks. His
piercing eyes darted around the room constantly. His
appearance could only be described as disheveled. The light blue
shirt was too big and the tan pants were too small. His
noticeable stomach bulged over his belt causing it to disappear.

The computer science department meeting had been in
session for over two hours and he was feeling left out. He had
been doing email on the small laptop sitting in front of him
oblivious to the meeting. But now he was ready to be heard.
Gerry was twice as big as any of the other six people in the
meeting. He raised his pudgy hand and waved it frantically at
Robert Snow, the man in charge of the Computer Science
department and Gerry's boss. Robert, who was tall and slim,

continued to make his points about the goals for the coming year and areas where improvements were needed.

Shit this guy is never going to stop and let me say something. How did I end up in this crap job? And those idiotic Windows PCs. Crappiest computers I've ever seen. I can see why I can't keep the students I need to work on them. The problems are endless.

Gerry thought about other jobs that he had coveted and applied for. He had seen enough computer rooms and been on-call too many times. He had paid his dues. No more pizza and coke all-nighters to fix computer problems for him. He was ready for management. But, for some reason he couldn't land the job he wanted. Most of the openings in computer-related management jobs were for businesses that used Microsoft products. Almost all personal computers used some version of Windows and many of the servers used NT. He had no desire to learn or even be around non-UNIX computers. And, most of the time he could not hide that fact. The last interviewer told him that he needed more Microsoft operating system experience to be given the job. He walked out in disgust. There is nothing he hated more in the world than Microsoft operating systems.

"Hey Bob. I have a question," interrupted Gerry.

Robert Snow, who emanated acute intelligence, finally looked up at Gerry who was now tense as indicated by his bright red ears and neurotic stare. The others cringed and waited hoping that this did not mean that the meeting would drag on. It would not be the first time.

"Gerry, I was just going to talk about your department. I guess I might as well start now," said Robert.

"But, but…" said Gerry with clenched fists.

"Hold on Gerry! You can ask questions when I'm done," glared Robert.

Although he lost none of his childish intensity, Gerry pulled his hand back and tried to act like he was listening.

"As you all know, our students and faculty are dependent on computers. So, our support of those computers is a key element in our mission statement. I know most of you are concerned more with teaching, but we have found out the hard way that having non-functional computers can be disastrous. More than ever networking and internet access is crucial. Don't you agree, Gerry?" asked Robert.

"Uh, uh, yes Bob. That's very true." said Gerry.

Robert sat up straight making him seem to grow even taller as he stared at the huge, red-faced IT manager. Gerry fidgeted in his undersized chair.

"This year we have to do better with our support. There were too many problems that were not resolved fast enough and some still have not been resolved. We need to see improvement, Gerry."

"But, but, I have to use students. I only have one other paid technologist to help me," whined Gerry.

"You know that we don't have any more money to pay for outside help. You will have to do the job with the resources we have here on campus. I won't accept that as an excuse," said Robert.

"Well it would be a lot easier if we didn't have all of those crappy Windows PCs to deal with. Have you considered my suggestions?"

"I don't want to hear one more word about getting rid of Windows. We've been over this. Windows is here to stay, no matter what you think of it. With that I'm ending this meeting. Enjoy the rest of the day everybody."

Gerry looked to the ceiling in disgust and shook his head. He almost screamed at Robert Snow who was walking through the doorway. *Stupid Windows, stupid boss*, he thought.

~~~

Gerry's large pudgy fingers pounded on the keyboard causing it to bounce off the desk as he typed. Various frames of text and pictures appeared on his computer screen only to disappear to be replaced by different data streams. Unlike his work office, this room in his small home was a mess, with stacks of paper strewn around in between new and old computer equipment. Wires were everywhere. As usual Gerry was engrossed in the cyber world that he craved and loved.

A light tap came on his shoulder. He looked up to see his girlfriend who was also rather large with stringy brown hair. She wore blue jeans and a T-shirt with little makeup.

"Uh hi Tessa. I was just getting into a chat room. What do you need?" asked Gerry who started to get up.

Tessa moved back slightly. Her eyes reflected nervousness and her lips were clamped together. Gerry waited to see what she wanted but was aching to get back to his computer.

"Don't get up. This won't take long. I know we don't talk much but I thought about our last talk. I've decided to move out," said Tessa.

"What? I thought we were good. You don't need to leave," said Gerry.

"I know you thought we were good. That's part of the problem. Maybe you're good but this isn't working for me. I like computers but with you it's an obsession. I need a boyfriend."

"Hey, I can do better. Give me a chance, baby."

15

"What about a family and marriage? Have you thought about that?"

"Uh, er, uh. Not really. Don't you think it's a little soon for all that?"

"I'm going to pack my stuff. I can stay with my sister in Seattle for a while."

Gerry looked at her. She seemed determined and the mention of marriage had shaken him. He didn't want to get into a conversation about marriage and having a family. He decided pleading with her to stay would be counterproductive.

"Uh, if that's what you really want. I'm just sorry it had to be this way."

Tessa turned toward the door as tears started forming in her sad brown eyes.

"Me too, me too," she mumbled.

Gerry's head snapped back to the computer screen and his pudgy fingers flew across the keyboard. Soon he was lost in cyberspace and Tessa was far from his thoughts.

Chapter 4

------**Email**-------
From: Strong, Amy[AmyStrong@WWU.edu]
To: O'Brien, Kelly[Kellyobrien@UW.edu]
Subject: Soccer

Hi Kelly
I luv how Colt is so supportive. Especially with my soccer. He comes to a lot of my practices, even. I wonder if he thinks about playing? I bet he was really good.
Amy

------**Email**-------

Colt heard the cheers of a huge crowd before anything came into view. The rumble of the cheering made his body vibrate with goose-bump ecstasy. Then, in an instant, he was running across a rich green soccer field with an eternal sun penetrating his soul. The vibrant, green grass was like a living, mindful carpet that responded to his every step. He floated across it, with ease and authority. The crowd roar became distant as he digested the rich colors and ethereal warmth coming into him. Non-descript opponents flew past as if within a virtual game world. *Where is the ball, where is the ball*, he thought. It was a query that moved him forward but did not reflect extreme desire. It was merely the obvious question. No urgency was attached.

Now a round purple and red soccer ball appeared at his feet as he ran. Its colors were scintillating and deep. He continued to glide forward as players attempted to distract him from the

17

goal. Each was dispatched and washed away in his wake. It felt like the bright globe was a part of him that could not be detached by any external force. His excitement increased as he saw open field in front of him. A newfound strength propelled him toward the net. He circled to the right and kicked. The ball shot from his foot leaving a quasi-rainbow that prominently displayed lilac purple, mixed with pinkish red trailing behind. As the orb penetrated the net, Colt felt and saw the smiling, oval face of his girlfriend Amy, and felt happiness wash over him. Then he woke to the jarring sounds of a human voice.

"Hey Colt, are you awake now?" asked Bobby Jones

A disoriented Colt looked up at his friend. *Damn, why did he need to wake me up? I was really enjoying that dream."*

"Uh sorta," said Colt.

"You wanted me to wake you up. Remember?"

"Er, uh, I did?"

"The practice. Amy's practice," said Bobby.

"Oh. What time is it?" said Colt

"It started a half hour ago."

"Crap, I better get going, then. Dude, thanks for waking me up, even if I didn't like it."

Still, Colt closed his eyes to absorb the feelings that the dream had induced. After a few seconds he managed to get moving. He jumped up and pulled on some gray sweatpants, old day-glo red tennis shoes and a pink t-shirt. Then he was gone.

The practice field was wet and somewhat muddy after an earlier downpour. Small puddles were evident across the expanse. Billowy, majestic, white clouds hung overhead. It was late afternoon. A scrimmage was in progress with eight girls to a side. One team wore deep blue pullover practice shirts and the other wore white. A section of the field was designated for the scrimmage to allow another group to run drills in at the opposite end.

Colt arrived gasping for air after sprinting all the way from his dorm room. When his breathing slowed down, he trotted briskly up and down the sideline clapping his hands while watching the young women but most of all Amy. It was obvious that this group was experienced and focused. Every player was athletic, disciplined and physical. The girls were working together, shouting, and seemed to be enjoying themselves. Coaches would stop play at times to explain, criticize or encourage a player. One theme pervaded all practices that Colt had attended. Every coach told the girls to be physical. Colt had seen that if a fight broke out they looked the other way for a short amount of time before breaking it up. At first he couldn't believe what they were doing, but over time he saw that college soccer was very physical. *I hope a few of these dudettes get into it. A fight in the mud would be awesome.* Colt saw Amy running toward the sideline where he had stopped to watch. The ball came to her. She kicked it up the sideline near him and slowed, looking for an opening. A smaller girl on the opposite team came at her, attacking the ball. Amy smiled at Colt and stopped abruptly, causing the defender to slide past her and fall down in the mud. Amy passed the ball to a teammate and continued up the field. *Man, is she good*, thought Colt. *Really good.*

Watching Amy along with her teammates brought a longing to Colt. He was proud of her but also a little jealous. He looked at the white line separating him from the field and sensed that it was a deep, vast chasm, even though it was but a few inches wide. He remembered and regretted his decision, many years ago, to stop playing the sport he loved. The desire to be running up and down the field was like a tidal wave building inside him that surged of its own accord. Colt closed his eyes and thought, *damn I never should have quit. Crap, I probably wouldn't have been that great anyway. I guess I'll never know.* Then he remembered his dream and had a vision of himself kicking the ball past a nondescript goalie for a score. Although it was now years in the past, he still remembered the feeling of scoring after extended periods of extreme effort.

Something hit Colt in the back returning him to reality. He spun and saw a white and black soccer ball at his feet. Before he had time to think about it, he kicked the ball and raced down the sideline toward the end of the field. It exhilarated him to experience the feel of a soccer ball under his feet again. He lost a sense of himself and his emotional baggage, giving him feelings of soaring above everything. After he returned the ball to the two girls who were waiting for him, tears started to well in his eyes. *I have to get out of here before I start blubbering all over myself. Geez, I didn't see this coming.*

Later in the day Colt and Amy went to the cafeteria and had coffee. Colt remembered how being on the field had affected him. He tried to put it out of his mind.

"I saw you running with the ball. You looked okay for a computer guy," teased Amy.

"Uh, well, I guess I just remembered what it was like," said Colt.

"Maybe you should do some rec soccer. I think they have a league here on campus."

Colt thought that he would enjoy soccer for fun but doubted it was possible.

"Nah, that's over for me. Anyway, I don't have time to do anything as it is."

She leaned over and kissed him and then whispered in his ear.

"You looked really sexy. It got me going a little bit."

Colt looked at her and saw that she was blushing. Her bright blue eyes were slightly glazed over. He whispered back.

"I'm sure we can do something about that. Let's go to my room."

Amy smiled and started loping swiftly toward the exit. Colt scrambled to catch her as she giggled with glee.

Chapter 5

------Email-------
From: Carbon, Matthew[MatthewC@hocs.biz]
To: O'Brien, Colt[ColtOB@yahoo.com]
Subject: School

Hi Colt
A little advice:

Education is a key to your future success. There are many distractions in college
life that can keep you from the goal. The easiest bad habit to fall into is to go to
parties often and ignore schoolwork. Avoid this.

Passing the certification exam is a great achievement. However, you still need to
learn more and gain experience. I suggest you continue your certification studies
and be open to gaining experience from hard work.

Lastly, I hear that you will be joining the computing support team at Western. I
know Gerry Lathrop a little. He is a bright guy but is mainly focused on UNIX.
Since your background is in Windows watch out. He thinks anything relating to
Windows is for losers.

Feel free to contact any of us in the program. We are rooting for your success.

Matthew

------Email-------

The late summer sunlight reflected from bright green
leaves, giving the Western University campus a subtle radiance.
Colt felt energetic but calm, as he walked to his meeting with
Gerry Lathrop, the head of computing support. This
environment nourished him as much as food and sleep. It was

as if the grounds of Western filled up his psychic reservoir, giving him an inner feeling of strength and purpose. *I wonder why I feel so laid back and hopeful here? It sure feels like this place is special.*

As he neared a large oak tree, Colt felt a persistent, magnetic pull in his mid-section. He veered toward the majestic tree to take a closer look. *This might be interesting.* A simple white, cement bench was next to the oak. *That bench, it seems like I belong there.* Colt sat and quickly slipped into a meditative state. Even though his eyes were open, vivid images moved across his inner field of vision. One image continued to flash by until Colt was able to focus and keep it in one place. It was an oil lamp similar to one in the stories about genies and magic carpets. The lamp was bright blue which seemed odd to Colt. *Wow, I thought those lamps were always gold. This one is a lot different. Maybe there is a genie in there who will grant me wishes?*

The next thing Colt remembered was walking toward his meeting with Gerry Lathrop. The memory of the blue lamp was quickly fading into the past as he mentally prepared for the first meeting with his new boss. One outcome, of his detour, was an overwhelming curiosity about what was to come. He had read the email from Mr. Carbon and had many questions about this new world he was to enter. *Hmmm. I wonder if this dude is alright? I want someone who will help me get better. Why would he think Windows is for losers? What the hell is UNIX. Is that like a MAC? I guess I'll find out soon enough.*

After wandering the halls of a large building, Colt found the office of the head of computer support. He knocked on the solid wooden door.

"Come in," said a pleasant voice

Colt opened the door and was surprised to see an organized office. *Where is all the computer stuff?* Photographs hung on the wall. There were a few filing cabinets but little else. A slim computer monitor sat on top of the solid wooden desk. Colt noticed the desk because most of the desks he had seen were made out of flimsy particle board or plastic. It gave the room a sense of permanence. All of a sudden a large man was grabbing Colt's hand and shaking it with vigor. The handshake sent subtle signals to Colt's inner self. *Man, this guy has some nervous energy. He's like a football player before a big game.* Although Colt was sturdily built, Gerry Lathrop seemed like a giant next to him. After he regained his composure, Colt looked at his new boss. He was as tall as Colt's friend Bobby but that is where the resemblance ended. Gerry was not only tall, but also wide and heavy. His white face was accented by bright red cheeks. Although he was energetic for a big man, he did not have the grace of an athlete.

"Er, uh, hi Mr. Lathrop. I'm Colt O'Brien" said Colt.

"Hellooo Colt. You can call me Gerry" said Gerry with a big smile.

Colt wondered if that smile was real as he tried to figure out what was going on in Gerry's head. Gerry walked back to his desk, sat down and indicated to Colt to sit in a nearby chair. Colt was now able to get a good look at his new boss. Colt saw that Gerry was a large man in his mid 30s. Colt guessed that he was six feet four inches tall and weighed in at close to 300 pounds. His most noticeable trait was a large, round, shiny bald head. Gerry's bright blue eyes never stopped moving. Colt guessed that when he started to speak his arms would gesticulate, expressing the nervous energy behind the facade. *I bet this guy eats lots of pizza. He's like a whale on his third espresso.*

"I read your note. It looks like there is a lot of work to do here," said Colt.

"Well, I have more work than I have people to do it. We need skilled individuals like yourself," said Gerry

Colt noticed that his arms were making wide movements that seemed bigger than the words being said.

"What will I be doing? I know about Windows, mostly," said Colt

"Almost all of our students use Windows. We have a hot line where they can call in trouble tickets when they have problems. And, we see every kind of problem, Hardware, software, you name it."

"So, I'll be helping fix PC's then?" asked Colt.

"Eventually you will. I have a project that has been sitting on the backburner waiting for someone to work it. I think you'll be perfect."

When he said perfect, Gerry raised both of his hands and formed circles with the thumb and forefinger of each. As this happened, Colt saw the image of the blue lamp, he had seen earlier at the oak tree, flash across his inner mindscape. Smoke floated out of the lamp forming a large blue cloud. As the smoke cleared the face of Gerry was revealed. The face had a mischievous grin. Colt sensed that Mr. Lathrop was like the genies he remembered from fairy tales. *Oh yeah. This guy will grant me some wishes but he has some tricks up his sleeve. No way I can trust big boy Gerry.*

"What is the project?" asked Colt.

"Why don't you settle in and get acclimated. I'll tell you what I need in a week or so," said Gerry.

Man, that smile is scary. It's like he is selling me a used car with no brakes.

"I'll do whatever you need. I hope it's a Windows thing," answered Colt

"Do you only know Windows? My background is UNIX. That's a real operating system. Do you have any experience with UNIX?" asked Gerry.

"Only know about Windows. I still have a lot to learn."

"Well maybe we can convert you. Let's see how it goes."

When he said that, Colt could see an arrogant glint in his eyes. *Man this guy is really down on Windows. I wonder what he has in mind for the new Windows guy? Ahhhhhhh!*

"I better head out. I'll wait to hear from you, then" said Colt

"It was great meeting you Colt. This is going to be fantastic. I will contact you in a week or so.

"Thanks. See ya later," said Colt.

As soon as Colt left Gerry's office he started to see visions of Gerry the genie playing tricks on him. Gerry would be visible and then disappear. His countenance would change from happiness bordering on ecstasy to dark brooding depression.

What the hell am I in for? Who is this genie man, really? I feel storm clouds forming in my future. Geez.

Chapter 6

------Email-------
From: O'Brien, Colt[ColtOB@WWU.edu]
To: Jones, Bobby[Bobbyj@WWU.edu]
Subject: Users

Dude
Users are weird. Too many stupid problems. Too many brain-dead Dudes and Dudettes.
And Dude, these UNIX guys are really out there. I need a Windows guy on my side. You up for it?

Later

------Email-------

Colt walked with quickness and determination into the central WWU tech room. His attire reflected a need to excel on his first day of working trouble tickets. He wore a bright Day-Glo purple sweatshirt with red and blue tie-die slacks and pink tennis shoes. It was topped off with a Microsoft baseball style cap. Over his shoulder was a bulging computer bag, His laptop, tools and software disks were inside. *This will be great. Finally, I 'm ready to kick ass,* he thought.

Colt recalled what he had just gone through to even be able to work trouble tickets. The project that Gerry had mentioned in their first meeting was messy, tiring and frustrating. Numerous network rooms were in extreme disarray with wires strung in all directions, extra equipment lying around and just general messiness. Colt's task was to make order out of years of accumulated chaos. Since he had little experience with wiring and network equipment, he tried to learn from the other technologists in his group. Nobody had a plan, information or encouragement. He resorted to reading books and asking anybody that might be able to help him. After a crash course and on the job trial and error, he was able to slowly finish the project. It was like walking the gauntlet and coming out the other side bruised and bloodied. When it was over he knew that this was his initiation into the tech group. He doubted that anyone was willing to do what he did.

Now he was enthused about moving forward and doing what he was good at. *Let's get to the real work.* A short, slim, pasty-faced student approached. The student's primary trait was geekiness. He lacked any physical presence. In his hands were a pager, cell phone and sheets of white paper which he handed to Colt. The pager was vibrating persistently.

"Hi Colt, I'm Bradley. This is your stuff."

Colt looked around the large room that, to him, seemed to be in complete disarray. *I guess those dirty wiring rooms aren't the only messes around here.* Computers, laptops, stacks of boxes of assorted parts and boxes of software littered the area. Printers and other assorted devices were mixed in. Instead of boxes of paper being stacked in one place they were scattered around the room. *Crap, I feel like organizing this place before I trip over something. Even the Highline tech room wasn't this bad.* Two twenty-something girls dressed in t-shirts and shorts sat staring at flashing computer screens. They wore telephone headsets and were talking non-stop. They seemed bored, frustrated and a bit drained.

"Okay. So what is the plan, dude?" asked Colt,

Bradley did not answer but looked at Colt from head to toe with slight disdain. After looking skyward, he spoke.

"You get text pages with tickets. You fix the problem and close the ticket."

"How do I do that?" asked Colt who was starting to get a queasy feeling.

"You log on the tech web site and close the ticket. Some instructions and account information are on the sheets that I gave you."

"So, that's it? Just me and the users?"

"Yeah, it's just windows stuff. How hard can it be?"

What the hell. Is this nerd nuts, or what?

"Oh, so you know windows stuff? You think it's easy?" asked Colt, who was starting to become irritated.

An expression of extreme arrogance came over Bradley's pale pimply face. Colt's inner radar sensed extreme irritation bordering on hatred emanating from the student.

What's up with this dork? Why is geeky boy so uppity?

"No way I do Windows. I do UNIX," snarled Bradley.

Colt was taken by surprise at Bradley's reaction. He wasn't aware that he had that much energy to exert.

Ooohhhh, I guees this guy is alive! A UNIX guy, thought Colt. *I didn't think they would be this stuck up.*

"Okay, Brad. I get it. You're a UNIX guy. Are there any windows guys around here?"

"Our network and servers are all UNIX. Only the PCs are Windows. So, we don't have many Windows techs. And...my name is Bradley."

I have a really bad feeling about this. UNIX, UNIX everywhere. This twerp is getting on my nerves already.

"I thought you had some NT servers, too?"

"Just a few test servers that we hardly use and I hope never get into production," said Bradley.

"How about this, Bradley? You give me the short version of the whole process before I start?"

Bradley heard his name being spit out of Colt's mouth and he lost some of his disdainful attitude. He also noticed that Colt wasn't impressed or afraid of him.

"Uh, er, yeah. Well, it's really not too complicated. A student or teacher has a computer problem and they call the help line. Those girls over there take the call and try to fix the problem over the phone. If they can't fix it, they type in a ticket and it goes out to the pager. You work on the problem. Once the problem is fixed, you log on to the web site and close the ticket.

"Well, gee, Brad. That wasn't so hard was it? So if that's all, I guess I'll sit around waiting for tickets?" said Colt

"There are a few tickets already on your pager. You can get started now."

"Well, now that I think of it, you better introduce me to whoever I need to know. I should probably know the girls at least."

After a reluctant Bradley introduced Colt to some of his co-workers and answered a few more questions, it was time to move on to the next thing.

"I better start doing trouble tickets. Later," said Colt.

I better get away from this guy before I pop him in the nose. Little piss-ant. I wonder if they'll give me a laptop to use. I guess I can use my stuff for now.

After the shock of being treated like a leper, the next surprise was the list of tickets displayed in text on his pager. Once he fiddled around with the buttons, he found that there were over ten tickets to work. *Shit, am I the only guy that works this stuff?* After a few hours of trying to get into the flow of working computer problems, Colt's frustration level was high and his patience was low. Everything was new; the building locations, the ticketing system, the computer network and it seemed like a million other things. *Damn, these guys sure know how to welcome a new guy. Just throw him into the toilet and flush.* He had changed the pager setting to "beep" mode and the shrill "beep, beep, beep" of his pager seemed to be un-ending. In the middle of fixing one problem two more pages would come in. Each page displayed a text message that had more information about the problem than Colt cared to see. To him, most of it was useless. Also, working alone on the first day was frustrating. He felt like a rudderless boat in a stormy sea. The users and their computer problems were varied and numerous. Many of them seemed more interested in getting in his way than having the problem resolved. *Crap, I just don't fix problems, I also have to comment and close tickets, call in and whatever other stupid thing they want. And the users. Am I a baby sitter or what? Ahhhhhh!*

Colt was looking at wires connected to a PC when his cell phone rang. He frowned and answered.

"Yeah".

"Hi Colt what's happening? Why are you so behind on the tickets?" said his new boss, Gerry.

Gerry sounded irritated which seemed unjustified to Colt. He cringed and bit his tongue. His frustration was boiling over like foamy, poison brew from a witch's cauldron. He wanted to lash out at someone, anyone. He hated failure. He hated not having all the answers. Most of all, he hated being treated like a leper by Bradley the UNIX geek. The work was not all new to him but this sort of treatment was. *This is not fair. These guys just throw me out there with no prep and no help. Screw them. This guy Gerry is either stupid or he's out to make me look bad. The son of a bitch. I'll give him a piece of my mind,* thought Colt. As Colt prepared to blast

Gerry Lathrop with both barrels, he realized he should step out of the dorm room.

"Uh, give me a minute," said Colt.

As Colt walked toward the door, he distinctly heard a voice. It said "Don't step into the trap." He looked both ways, down the hall he was now standing in, and behind, but saw no one. His anger changed into curiosity, as he thought, *who was that?* Then he remembered Gerry Lathrop waiting on the other end of the line. *Crap, I guess I better watch out for old Gerry the genie.*

"Uh, sorry about that, Gerry. I had to step into the hall. What was the question?" said an apologetic Colt.

"What is taking so damn long getting the trouble tickets complete? What's the problem?" said Gerry.

I can't go at this guy directly. That's what he wants. If I've learned anything it's that the dude who loses his cool goes down in flames.

"Er, uh ya know, I feel bad about that but I guess I need to adjust to this new job. There are a lot of different things to learn. I'm trying my best."

"We thought you were supposed to know all of this stuff," said Gerry.

Colt could feel Gerry's imperious attitude bearing down on him. After a brief battle with his emotions, Colt responded.

"I know I'm new and it will take time, but I have done nine tickets so far. At least that's something. It seems like a lot of tickets just keep coming in. How many trouble tickets do the other Windows guys get done?" asked Colt.

The line was silent for about twenty long seconds. Colt sensed that he had hit a weak spot. *At least he shut up for a minute.*

"Oh, uh, er, er.., you've closed nine tickets in a few hours?" asked Gerry.

He is back-pedaling. Time to push a little.

"Yeah, Gerry. And, I have about six more on my pager. How many people does it usually take to get that many done?"

"Never mind then. Just remember that you have to do better. We need the best support. Our students need their computers up and running."

Then Colt saw a vision of a genie version of Gerry Lathrop turning into smoke and getting sucked back into the blue lamp.

"I have tickets to work, Gerry. Is that all?" said Colt

"Yes, that's all. Goodbye."

Yeah, go back and hide in your lamp, genie man. I'm sick of your crap.

After a grueling first day, when Colt got to his dorm room, he called Amy who came over immediately. When he told her about his day, she was sympathetic and a little irritated.

"I can't believe that they treated you like that. Am I ever going to see you with all that work you have to do? Why don't you just get away from that?" she asked.

"I can't. It's part of my scholarship," moaned Colt.

"I'm getting mad. How about this? You lie down and I'll give you a massage?

Colt slumped on the small bed and Amy gently rubbed his shoulder and back. After a few minutes Colt was sound asleep.

Chapter 7

------Email-------
From: O'Brien, Colt[ColtOB@WWU.edu]
To: O'Brien, Leona[LeonaB@aol.com]
Subject: School

Hi Mom
I thought I would send email instead of a call. I expected to be busy at college but this is crazy. Between schoolwork, fixing computers and everything else, Im overloaded. I guess I will get used to it but it seems impossible. I miss having my own room at home. This dorm living is crap. At least I will be down there soon. See you then.

Love
Colt
------Email-------

Colt and Amy strolled along a side street in Bellingham. They stopped occasionally to peer into a shop window. It was an early fall Saturday and the sun was shining through cool, crisp, sea air. Neither of the two seemed interested in a final destination. Amy grabbed Colt's arm and pulled him close. It was Amy's idea to get away from the campus and meet Bobby Jones for lunch. She had been hearing rumors about Bobby that seemed inconsistent with his past behavior and personality. As Colt had said many times, 'Bobby is the dude who never does anything wrong'. Now, Amy's friends, on the soccer team, were telling her a different story. They said that Bobby was at all the parties and he wasn't sitting on the sidelines. Also, he seemed to be very interested in girls no matter what background or habits. One girl told Amy that she felt someone grabbing her butt at a party and turned to see Bobby smiling sheepishly. *I have find out what's going on with Bobby*, thought Amy. *What I'm hearing is too weird.*

"It's nice to just wander around and not think about anything." said Amy.

"Yeah, my brain needs to settle. I have so much stuff flying around in my head that it's hard to keep it all straight," said Colt.

"So where are we meeting Bobby again?" asked Amy.

"Uh, it's a small place a couple of blocks up."

"How is it going with him? I'm hearing really funny stuff. It's like they're talking about another person."

Colt steered Amy toward a low wall overlooking the ocean below. They settled in as Colt gathered his thoughts. After gazing at the sea for a bit, Colt spoke.

"You know I hate this dorm living. And, Bobby isn't making it any better. He's messy. I never see him cracking a book when he's there which isn't very often. I've heard stories about kids coming to college and they crash and burn. I don't want to get into his business, but I think he's going down fast."

"Maybe we can help him? Have you said anything to him?" asked Amy.

"Not really. It's like I don't exist to him. Anyway, I have enough crap to deal with. I can see how dudes fail. It's a big change. I've been just trying to survive everything," said Colt.

"Well, we have about a half hour before we're supposed to meet him. Let's walk around and think of what we can do."

"Okay, but let's go easy. You know, feel him out. He's the last guy I thought would let things get to him," said Colt.

"Does he have a girlfriend?"

"I think he has figured out that he really likes girls but I don't think one girl is what he is looking for. And, I think he is drinking now. Sometime he smells like booze in the morning."

"Okay, let me just talk to him first. I want to get a feeling about what's going on with him."

"Uh okay," said Colt.

As they strolled Amy made sure that they always had a view of the water. Somehow it was soothing to both of them. Colt thought about his friend and the changes he noticed. He thought he knew Bobby very well, but living with him was an eye-opener. His friend seemed to have changed overnight. *That dude really is different. I guess I'm so into my own thing that I have a hard time keeping up with his life. Maybe Amy can get him to open up and we can figure out what's going on?*

Eventually, Colt and Amy arrived at the small café named Clancy's. It featured American food with breakfast all day. *At least it isn't some fufu, hippy, herbal tea place,* thought Colt. They sat and both ordered coffee. After scanning the menu for awhile, Colt was becoming impatient.

"I wonder where he is? He's already fifteen minutes late," said Colt.

"Give him some more time Colt. Try to relax," said Amy.

Colt was still wondering where this meeting was headed. It was difficult for him to decide how to approach his friend. *I'm getting too jacked up about this. I might just slap him up side of the head. I guess I better let Amy talk?* After another 20 minutes and three cups of coffee, Bobby eased up to the table and sat down. His face was pale and he seemed sleepy. His eyes had a vacuous look when they could see them. Bobby avoided direct eye contact. He appeared even skinnier than usual to Colt. Amy got a sense that Bobby was empty, like a hollow tube. Both Amy and Colt noticed that he said nothing about being late. *Screw him,* thought Colt.

"Hey dude. How is it going? Are you hungry?" asked Colt.

Amy leaned into Colt in a subtle way, reminding him to be casual in his approach. He could feel tension in her demeanor. *I guess she can tell he is not looking very good, too. I feel like shaking the guy.*

"Yeah, let's eat something," said Bobby.

After ordering, Amy talked about general topics including studying, social relationships and her participation on the soccer team. Colt was irritated that Bobby said almost nothing in response but held his tongue in check. When the food came Colt attacked his plate while Amy and Bobby ate small amounts at a slow pace. Finally, Colt decided that this meeting was headed nowhere. He looked at Amy and could see she needed some help.

"So dude, are you feeling okay? You don't look hungry?" asked Colt.

"Uh, yeah, uh, I'm a little tired. I partied a little last night."

"Was it fun?" asked Amy.

"Yeah, I had a good time but now my head hurts," said Bobby.

"Was there anybody there that we know?" asked Amy.

Bobby started to look like a cornered rat. He closed his eyes as he tried to maintain some semblance of wakefulness.

"Uh, I don't remember that much about the party. I drank some beers and everything got sorta hazy after that."

Colt couldn't sit in silence another minute.

"Dude, what happened? It's like you forgot who you were," said Colt a more anger than he wanted.

A look of fear and irritation came to Bobby's face. Amy's hand grabbed Colt's arm and squeezed.

"Hey, I'm okay. I just like to blow off some steam once in awhile. And, I like meeting girls. What's wrong with that?" asked Bobby.

37

"Do you even go to class? Right now I can see that you're hung over," said Colt.

Bobby stood up to leave with his fists clenched.

"We're just worried about you," said Amy.

"You don't need to worry about me. I'm fine. Stay out of my life," said Bobby as he walked away.

Tears formed in Amy's bright blues eyes.

"Why can't we just care what happens to him?" she sobbed.

Colt hugged her and said nothing.

When Colt returned to his dorm room, Bobby was gone. Colt studied late into the night but his friend did not return. The next morning Bobby was still gone. Colt grimaced. *I have a bad feeling that he went out boozing after our talk. I guess we won't try that again for awhile.*

Chapter 8

------**Email**-------
From: Anonymous, Mr.[mranon@anonymous.net]
To: Freeman, John[freebird@anonymous.org]
Subject: Do you think he'll buy it?

Hey

I think I'm ready for the meeting. I have the list of questions. Do you really think that the changes we discussed will get his attention? I sent him my proposal last week. Do you think he'll agree to do it? I guess I'll find out at the meeting.

F

------**Email**-------

    Malcolm Bates sat in his spacious, immaculate office with a large, thin monitor beaming light into his face. It was almost dark outside and rain was pelting the large windows that faced the Puget Sound in the Seattle skyscraper where he sat. He liked to keep the office lights off when concentrating on important information. Working into the night was the norm rather than the exception. He was accustomed to late hours and appreciated having no distractions with the office empty and only a few emails trickling in. Like many IT managers he was dressed casually in spite of his position in the company. He wore brown slacks and a light blue shirt. The one extravagant item in his apparel was a Hublot MDM watch that he wore on his right wrist. It was a symbol of his success and had been given to him along with almost two million shares of stock when his company went public.

This proposal needed all of his attention as it entailed some risk but great potential rewards. The first phase of the massive software project, that he oversaw, was complete. It was an intricate system of smaller, linked programs that allowed large companies to manage all of the computers on their network centrally. The initial cost to the client was huge. The ongoing cost for maintenance and upgrades was also substantial. After years of development, the first version had been released only a few months ago. The initial reaction from customers was positive but that was to be expected. Most early buyers were also beta-testers for the software and were familiar with it. Malcolm's focused mind knew that other software companies were also soon to release similar software or already had. Most of them were big names in the industry. As it had always been, his company needed to be noticeably better to compete. And, Malcolm needed to be somewhat paranoid concerning competitors. His primary focus in life was to maintain his competitive edge.

A young man sat waiting outside Malcolm's office. He looked like many programmers that worked in the Northwest. Little attention was paid to appearance. He was clean but, other than that, how he looked was not a priority, except to fit in with his small group of nerd pals. For the most part, he didn't care. Although he was starting to feel a strong attraction to girls, he did not equate appearance with success in that area. With long blond hair flowing down to his shoulders, he wore a T-shirt, shorts and tennis shoes without socks. The pouring rain was of little concern since there was parking in the building. He avoided Seattle when possible as he preferred more of a rustic setting. When he went outside, which was rare, he liked a serene, natural environment.

The empty waiting area gave him an eerie feeling. Being in a skyscraper was foreign enough to the thin, skittish computer whiz. But, being in an almost empty building made him more nervous with each passing second. His mind was racing as he pored over each detail of a printout of the proposal he submitted to Malcolm Bates. Although he had serious doubts about the possibility for success, his close friends were positive that what he was offering was what Malcolm needed. Just as he was reading a list of potential questions that might be asked with possible answers, he was startled by the door opening. He saw a man who carried himself like someone who was in charge. But, he also sensed a person who liked people and interacting with them.

"Hi, I'm Malcolm," he said with his hand out.

The programmer tried to calm down but remained antsy. He shook the executive's hand with a brief smile.

"Uh, er, hi," replied the nervous hacker.

The guest noticed that unlike many people he encountered, Malcolm treated him as a professional which put him at ease.

"I'm excited to discuss your proposal. Come into my office," said Malcolm with a smile.

The young man sat facing preoccupied executive and waited. He was happy to have a short window of time to scan the question and answer sheet for the hundredth time. After the Malcolm reviewed his notes and the information on his computer screen, he spoke.

"Well, I have to say that you seem to be reading my mind. We are a small and young company. So it can be challenging to do everything that we want in-house."

"I just thought that I could do some of the work for you."

"Of course, I made some inquiries about you. Everybody says the same thing. You're really good but usually work alone. Also you don't seem to have much of a resume," said Malcolm.

"Well, I'm just getting started," he answered.

"Well, some members of my team hold you in high regard."

"Did you like my proposal?" asked the programmer.

"Just so we're clear. What you will do for us is write software for our management system, do all the testing and deliver it to us. And, you can do this is less than a year," stated the executive.

"Uh yeah. That's the short version,"

"Because of the recommendations, I'm going to believe that you can do this work or at least give it a good try. What do you need? Where would you work?"

"I need computers. I need two desktops and two laptops along with some peripheral equipment. Also, I need access to the code that you currently have."

"What about compensation? And, you don't use Macs do you?"

"If I get the equipment, I won't need anything up front. I only use PCs with Windows. If you accept what I come up with, then I would like a good job and some stock," answered the nerd from his list of memorized answers.

"So you're saying that we don't give you anything except equipment. And. if we don't accept what you create then you get nothing?" asked Malcolm who remained skeptical about this arrangement.

"That's the deal."

"So where are you going to do the work?"

"Umm, uh, I need to figure that out. But, I won't need you to help with that."

Malcolm considered the unusual proposition again, wondering how this kid could come through without any money and no visible computer network to do the necessary testing. He also considered the items laid out in the proposal and marveled at the simple approach for providing all of the improvements to the program. He knew that someone close to the project team must have discussed the requirements with him. The proposal was actually an improvement over what his team was already working on. The main question to consider was how this work related to the in-house work that was already taking place.

The young programmer could almost see the wheels turning inside of Malcolm's head. After some time he started to anticipate disappointment. After all, who was he to be reaching so high? Yes, he was respected in his own group of hackers and programmers but why would a big-time exec take a chance with him. *Maybe this isn't going to happen. He's taking way too long,* thought the 21-year old.

Malcolm was serious as he spoke.

"Okay here's the deal. We are already doing some of this stuff. I will let you do your own thing with a few requirements. I want you to meet with my team lead, John Freeman. Go over what you're doing and keep him informed as you develop the programs. After two months you will submit what you have for us to look at. You will continue to do that as long as we say, with periodic submissions. We can terminate the agreement at any time," said Malcolm.

"What about the other stuff?" he asked with soaring expectations.

"We'll give you the equipment. If you give us good code as we go, we'll compensate you some but not a lot. At the end, if we accept and incorporate at least eighty percent of it into the application, I'll pay you twenty thousand shares of stock and a high-paying job."

"But I didn't ask for any money until I was done," said the surprised hacker.

"I'll feel better if you get compensated. So, if we use any of your work you got something. It will all be written up in the contract. Just remember, we own all of it. And, you don't get the stock and job unless we use most of what you give to us."

"Sounds good to me," smiled the young hacker.

The two shook and the young man almost skipped out the door. As he stood in the elevator he basked in the glow of his first big success. *I wonder if he knows that John Freeman is one of my buds. This is going to be too perfect. He would shit if he knew where I was going to do the testing.*

Chapter 9

```
------Email-------
From: Carbon, Matthew[MatthewC@hocs.biz]
To: Lathrop, Gerry[GerryLathrop@WWU.edu]
Subject: Colt O'Brien
----------------------------------------------------------------------
```

Hello Gerry

You may not remember, but we have met a few times in the past. I just wanted to put in a good word for Colt O'Brien. He was in our Microsoft Certification Program last year. He worked very hard to improve his skills. If you give him a chance, I am sure he will not disappoint. I have high hopes for Colt. If you have questions about Colt or if I can help in any way, let me know.

Regards
Matthew Carbon

------Email-------

Matthew Carbon sat at his desk thinking about Colt O'Brien and his situation at Western Washington University. He knew that Colt's boss, Gerry Lathrop was a "UNIX bigot" and had little respect for the Windows operating system. He saw Colt as a student who could pave the way for other students to follow if he was given a chance. He thought about an approach that would help Colt in his new environment. *I'll write Gerry Lathrop a note and see what happens. Maybe I can get some idea of how he will be dealing with his new student. The first year of college is hard enough without on-the-job hassles. If Colt needs help we can jump on it quickly, before it's too late.*

~~~

Gerry Lathrop stared at the computer screen in front of him in his well-organized campus office. The neatness of the large room belied the clutter of thoughts, images and emotional tides within his head. He was tense and a little bit irritated which was the norm. A list of unread emails was displayed on the screen. While he sorted through the list, wheels churned within his bright, manic mind. He tried to envision his computer networking department, at Western Washington University, running smooth like a new, high-priced automobile purring along on a test drive. He saw himself receiving accolades for a job well done from university administrators as he inspired his student employees into doing a stellar job. But, no matter how hard he tried, he could not keep reality at bay. He could not ignore the facts. The network servers and PCs had numerous problems that were difficult to impossible for his team of student workers to fix. His department was not able to keep up with the trouble tickets called in by teachers and students. He needed experienced professionals to work for him but had mostly inexperienced students. Also, his staff was on its own as far as training. Most of all, he needed highly technical individuals to work on the critical, complex problems that created crisis situations from time to time. No matter how well he and his team performed, one serious problem made all positive visibility disappear. And, the longer it took to fix the problem the worse he looked to his bosses.

Colt O'Brien was the one student who worked on broken personal computers running Windows. With the thousands of PCs at the university he was overwhelmed. Gerry hated Windows and people who worked on fixing Windows problems almost as much. *Windows is total crap*, he thought. *They never should have allowed that two-bit operating system onto my network. UNIX is the answer but they never even asked the right question.* Although Colt was doing a good job, it was impossible for Gerry to look at him as a real computer technologist. No one had ever done as many tickets as the young, confident student but still Gerry disliked and disrespected him. In spite of past experience with inept student workers, he couldn't help feeling that Colt could be replaced by almost anyone.

Gerry noticed a note from someone he did not recognize. *Who is that from,* he thought? He read the short note from Matthew Carbon. His mind started racing as his anger increased. *What a bunch of crap. Microsoft Certification has nothing to do with real computing. I can't believe anybody thinks it worth a shit. I don't even need to see how this kid does. He's worthless and so is his paper cert. As long as he is into Windows, he'll at most be average.*

A light knock came on the half-way open office door. Gerry looked up. *What is it now,* he thought. He saw that it was Bradley Tyler, his number one UNIX technician. The fragile, pasty-faced nerd slipped past the door. He seemed nervous.

"Hi Bradley," said Gerry.

"Hi Gerry," said Bradley.

Gerry smiled. "How are those UNIX servers running?"

"Uh, er, uh, fine. But that's not why I'm here," answered the geeky student.

"Let me guess. Is it something to do with Windows problems?"

"Yes, there are loads of Windows tickets. Colt is pretty good at working through them but there are too many for one person."

"They can't be that difficult to fix," stated Gerry with disdain.

"You are correct. Most of them aren't very hard. But, there are so many that once in a while there are tricky ones."

"So, what are you asking from me? Do you want to do some of those stupid tickets?"

"Uh, no, not me. I only do UNIX. But we could use one or two more techs for the Windows stuff."

"Can any of the guys we already have help out?" asked Gerry who just wanted Bradley with his Windows questions gone.

Bradley paused. He looked away trying not to show how nervous he was. The last thing he wanted was to work on personal computers that were using Windows. He had visions of being laughed at by other UNIX technologists.

"Uh, I don't think our UNIX guys have the time. And, I really think we need to work on complex UNIX problems," answered Bradley.

"I don't know if I see Colt O'Brien doing that great of a job. Let's watch him for awhile. Maybe he'll improve and start doing tickets faster. If not, I'm sure we can find someone else to fill his spot."

Bradley wondered who would fill in if Colt was gone. He worried that it might be himself.

"You really think so? He sure does a lot of tickets?" asked Bradley

"These Windows guys don't know much. They are wanabee technologists. Tell me how he is doing in a few weeks," smiled Gerry.

I know that kid bluffs his way through most of those tickets. There is no way he fixes that many real problems , thought Gerry.

Bradley walked down the hall shaking his head. He thought about working computer problems where he would deal with real people and not computers. *No way I want to do that*, he thought.

Chapter 10

------Email-------
From: Strong, Amy[AmyStrong@WWU.edu]
To: O'Brien, Kelly[Kellyobrien@UW.edu]
Subject: Family

Hi Kelly
With your soccer and school do you ever think about having a family? I know you will have lots of opportunities to work too. How will you deal with that?

Amy

------Email-------

Suzy Bower and Amy Strong sat at a tiny table in the Burien Starbucks. Both were sipping tall coffee drinks and talking at a rapid rate. Amy Strong was tall and athletic with an oval face. Her dark brown hair was pulled back into a ponytail making her sparkling, bright blue eyes stand out. Suzy Bower was in contrast to her friend in looks and personality. Her short black hair, deep brown eyes and attire gave her a sophisticated appearance. Where Amy was reserved, Suzy was outgoing. Amy was athletic and Suzy was more cerebral with a sarcastic sense of humor. Suzy was amazed by her best friend's outstanding soccer skills and competitive spirit. Whereas Amy could not understand how her friend moved through social situations with such ease.

"I like what you've done with your hair. It makes you look even more together," said Amy.

"I like how it turned out. I was hoping I might get noticed a little more by the guys. I'm looking but not finding," said Suzy.

"I guess I lucked out. Shy little me writes one email and finds the perfect guy. I thought it would be risky but it has been perfect so far."

Amy smiled as her eyes lost a little focus expressing a dreamlike quality.

"We all thought maybe he was a little too much for you but boy were we wrong. Sometimes it works that way I guess. Just not with me," whined Suzy.

"You are always getting asked out. What happens?" quizzed Amy.

"I get bored I guess. Maybe I'll do better in college. I sure hope so.

"So why are we going to see your friend, Julie?" asked Amy.

"Oh, I thought I told you. It's to see her new baby. She is so happy," said Suzy.

"Wow, I bet she is. Let's go. My latte is cold."

~~~

Amy and Suzy walked into the large living room where about ten young women were gathered. Suzy brightened noticeably as Amy tensed a bit. Most of the girls were in their twenties with a few older women in attendance. Since this was Normandy Park, many of the attendees were dressed formally with perfect makeup, shoes and outfits. Suzy took the lead. She and Amy were soon talking to a common acquaintance on the outside of the circle of interested young women surrounding the new mother and her baby boy. It was as if a huge invisible force was pulling all of them toward a center of indescribable joy. Julie held the baby in her arms and beamed. The baby smiled and seemed to enjoy all of the attention.

"That's Julie's sister next to her. Her name is Stacy. The baby's name is Scott," whispered Suzy to Amy.

"I can tell that the girls want to hold him. It's like they can't wait to get their hands on that kid," said Amy with a bit of reluctance in her voice.

Suzy raised her eyebrows and stared at her friend.

"Don't you want to hold him?" she asked.

Amy turned a bit red and looked away causing Suzy to wonder what was happening. Just at that moment the new mother passed the baby to her sister with an audible sigh. As each girl enjoyed holding the child, Julie talked about being a mother for the first time.

"I'm just so happy I have help. Todd is a great father. And my mother knows a lot. It's like non-stop work."

"Is he sleeping through yet?" asked a girl.

"Not yet. I get so little sleep that sometimes I can't tell if I'm awake or dreaming. That's one part of being a mother that is really hard," Julie replied.

The baby was now in Suzy's arms. It was making low pitched gurgling sounds and smiling with bright green eyes. Amy could feel the eyes of the group staring in their direction and knew that it was because of the baby. Amy had held babies before and knew how strong the attraction was. It was almost her turn but she was both attracted and afraid. Suzy leaned into her friend and started to pass the bundled child to Amy. Amy grimaced and froze. Suzy, who was becoming irritated, leaned over and whispered into Amy's ear.

"Take this baby, now."

Amy took the child. After adjusting her hold the baby felt snug in her arms. Now Amy felt like she was on stage as the others looked at her and Scott. She also sensed a longing to have a baby of her own rising up from deep inside. She was startled and scared.

Julie looked at Amy and said "You look comfortable holding that baby. Do you have any kids?"

"Uh no, not yet. I just started college." answered Amy.

Then, the baby gurgled again and smiled as Amy looked at him. When she saw the innocent child, it all seemed so natural, so comfortable. She wondered what it would be like to have a baby of her own. After thinking briefly about how much work a child would be, she envisioned herself with Colt and a newborn. *Oh my god, where is this coming from? I'm not ready for marriage and a family? Why am I thinking about having a baby now?*

The others in the room saw how Amy eased into a relaxed state as the infant fell asleep in her arms. Suzy could see that a woman with bright red hair next to Amy was wondering when her turn would come to hold the child.

"Maybe it would be good to let the others hold the kid?" whispered Suzy.

Amy who was still staring at Scott's hypnotic eyes said, "Uh, yeah, sure."

Amy had to make a conscious effort to disentangle herself from the cute, tiny human being. When she released the baby from her grasp she felt like a part of her had been severed and almost grabbed the child back. In a few minutes Suzy grabbed her friend's arm and led her toward the door.

"Calm down girl. Let's get out of here before you kidnap a baby," said Suzy.

Amy turned to look back with a longing stare as they exited into the pouring rain.

Chapter 11

------Email-------
From: Strong, Amy[AmyStrong@WWU.edu]
To: O'Brien, Kelly[Kellyobrien@UW.edu]
Subject: Student problems

Hi Kelly
I am really getting mad about this network job Colt has. It keeps
him away from me and now he is getting complaints from students.
Two sleazy girls tried to hit on him when he was fixing their
computers. Now, they are complaining after he told them to get
lost. What's next?
Arggghhhhh!
Amy

------Email-------

It was nearing lunch time. To Colt, the professor who was
speaking was boring. He droned on and on about how
computers functioned but knew almost nothing. Colt could not
believe how ignorant he was about even the basics of
computing. *I don't know how much more of this I can stand. What an
idiot.* The entire class was falling asleep. It was obvious to Colt
that most of the students knew more than the teacher. As he
started to raise his hand to say something, Colt's pager started
beeping. The text on the pager displayed SOS with ticket
information. As Colt was walking out of the classroom he
thought, U*h oh. Looks like about twenty PCs are screwed up. I better
get moving.*

After a short, rapid walk, Colt arrived at the dorm building indicated in the tickets. He took a brief look at one computer and realized that it was probably a network problem. He was able to run applications on the PC, but anything that required network connectivity, such as web browsing, did not work. *No wonder I have a lot of tickets. Maybe I can fix this and close all of the tickets at once.*

A young, hyper, male student hovered over Colt as he did his work. His name was Chet. To Colt, it felt like little short, intermittent blasts of electricity were hitting him. Colt was having difficulty keeping his focus.

He turned to Chet and said "Hey dude, could you give me a little room? I need to concentrate."

"Oh yeah, yeah, sure, ok" said the nervous student.

"What's so important?" asked Colt.

"Everybody is down. We need our email and the web," answered Chet.

"I'm going to unplug your PC and plug in my laptop. I can troubleshoot that way."

"Sure, sure…yeah. Just fix it."

Colt pulled his laptop out of his bag and plugged it in. He then inserted a software utilities CD. After starting a network utility and running some tests, he saw the cause of the problem. He typed in a command that displayed a list of numbers separated by periods.

"Got it," said Colt

"Got what?" said Chet.

"I have to go to another room one floor up. I'll come back after I fix the problem. Later, dude."

"But, but what….," asked Chet.

But Colt was gone. When he left the room he didn't take any of his equipment. He quickly found the room he was looking for and knocked on the door.

"Who is it?" said a timid, nervous, male voice.

"I'm with tech support. I need to look at your computer," said Colt

"Uh, why? I'm busy now," said the voice behind the door.

Colt was in no mood to argue. He suspected that this person's computer was hanging up the entire network in the building. *Screw this guy. I really don't need this crap.*

"The whole building is having network problems. I need to see what's going on. Open up or I'll call someone. Do you want that?" asked Colt.

"Uh, er, no man. You don't have to be so tense about it. Come on in."

Colt looked at the student who stood in the doorway. What he saw and felt was a smart, non-conformist. His face was pale with long, dishwater blond hair. He wore a flannel checked shirt, shorts and was barefoot. His gray piercing eyes were emanating nervousness and intelligence. Colt's inner radar sensed a high level of technical expertise from this thin, young man. However, he put up a front. He wanted to hide, to be invisible to others. Although Colt knew he was hiding something, he didn't know what.

"Let's take a look at your computer," said Colt

"Hey, I know a lot about computers. Mine are okay."

More than one computer? Hmm?

"How many computers do you have?" said a Colt.

As the student stepped aside Colt had his answer. In front of him were two desktop PCs and two laptops. Three huge monitors flashed text and images. Colt paused for a moment to ascertain the situation. His inner psychic vision displayed a large pipe with water rushing through it to this room, to these computers.

"Dude, I don't know what you are doing, but it's hosed up the whole building. Now, I can look at what you are downloading or you can stop it now. It's up to you," said Colt

"Uh, I'm sure it's not me. But, I can try some things to see if it helps."

"Do it fast or I'll need to take a look myself." said Colt with conviction.

The student jumped over to a keyboard while Colt watched. His fingers flew across the keys. In a few seconds all of the monitors went blank as all of the machines powered down. It was noticeable how quiet the little room became. Colt could still sense the large data pipe with his psychic vision. However, it now was almost empty. *Yeah, right. It's not his computer.*

"I think that fixed it," said Colt.

"I don't think it was my stuff," whined the student.

"Next time I will be looking at it myself. Then we will know for sure. With all of this hardware, I can see how you might overload things."

He noticed the student tensed and seemed to be pondering what to say. *I wonder if this guy is a hacker or what. Crap, I didn't even know that these little rooms had enough electricity to run this many devices.*

"Uh, can I get back to my life, now?" asked the student.

"Hey dude. Wait a minute. I'm Colt. I can see you know a lot about computers. Ever think about a job fixing them. I can sure use some help. "

"My name's Fletcher Rowe. I have enough stuff to do on my own equipment. Uh, er, thanks for asking, though," he replied.

Colt sensed that Fletcher wanted him out of the room before more questions were asked.

"Okay, dude. If you change your mind, here's my card. See ya later," said Colt.

After checking a few of the other computers in the building Colt called the help desk and asked one of the girls to close all of the tickets related to that building. He knew that the cause of the network problem was in the room with the four computers. *I wonder what that guy was doing. No way it was legal.*

~~~

After fixing the network problem, there was still one ticket on his pager. He was a bit proud of himself for being a hero and expected that this new problem would also result in a happy customer. However this situation was different, much different. Colt sat staring at the computer monitor. He was sitting in the dorm room of two sophomore girls. Darlene was thin with brown eyes and blonde hair and Selma was busty with black hair and light blue eyes. Both were giggling causing Colt to lose his concentration. Also, he could feel sexual tension in the tiny, enclosed area. Earlier, when he entered the messy dorm room it felt to him like he had walked into a misty cloud of female energy. The odor of various perfumes, lotions and other products assaulted his senses. The girls were friendly, too friendly. *I wonder if these two have been into the vino or maybe some weed?* It was as if both of them were angling to be close to him. They were constant chatterboxes with Colt in the middle of a machine-gun crossfire. After listening to the two talk about random topics, he was finally able to sit down and look at the first of two computers in the dorm room.

With some effort, Colt was able to get back on track and run software to clean the computer that was riddled with viruses, spyware and other assorted problems. After a short time, Colt no longer heard giggling or any other sounds coming from the frisky co-eds. *Maybe I can get this done and leave.* As he fixed each problem the computer increased in speed indicating that it was functioning better. When he started one last program, to finish the job, he could feel a presence on his right ear, then a whisper. As he heard the words, he also smelled the strong odor of wine.

"Colt, we really like you," whispered Selma in his ear.

Colt felt something on his shoulder and smelled perfume. He looked to see two large breasts rubbing up against him. They were covered with a flimsy, see-through material. Suddenly a large glass of red wine was placed in front of him. Then, in his left ear, he heard another whisper.

"Colt, why don't you relax a little? I think you need a massage and some wine," said Darlene in a sexy voice.

Colt could feel sensuous hands massaging his left shoulder. He was sandwiched between the two girls who were making their intentions known with each passing second. Before Colt could logically understand what was happening, he started to physically react to their attentions. Although he knew it wasn't right and that he should have more control, his body had other ideas. At the same time he had a vision of his girlfriend Amy. She was looking at him with angry eyes and a red face. *Crap, I better do something quick. This is screwed up.* Colt stood up and backed away from the girls. They both looked him up and down with a curious gleam in their eyes. He could not stop his eyes from gawking at their scantily clad bodies.

"Uh, I just remembered. I have to go to a meeting," said Colt.

"Oh, Colt. Don't leave us like this. We need your help," cooed Darlene.

"Don't you like my outfit?" teased Selma.

A war was now raging inside Colt. He knew that if he hesitated he would lose the battle and the war. He grabbed his laptop, threw it in his bag and headed for the door.

"Your computer is a lot better now. Nice meeting you. Bye," said Colt.

"But, what about the other computer?"

Colt turned, slammed the door behind him and sped down the hall. *Dude, that was close. That was really close. I thought I had more control than that.*

Chapter 12

------Email-------
From: O'Brien, Colt[ColtOB@yahoo.com]
To: Carbon, Matthew[MatthewC@hocs.biz]
Subject: I think I need some help

Hi Mr. Carbon
I think I need some help. Its really hard dealing with Gerry. I think he wants me to crash and burn. Can I call you?

Colt

------Email-------

Colt stood in front of two mirrors looking at himself. One reflected a clear image. He was smiling and confident. The other was blurry and disjointed. When he looked at the blurry image, Colt became uneasy, fearful and scatterbrained. *What the hell is happening to me? Why do I look like a blob of scattered colors? And, this weird feeling? What is that about?*

As he tried to understand, Colt thought of his boss, Gerry Lathrop. He knew that Gerry could not be trusted and was much like the mirrors in front of him. Gerry was clear or convoluted depending on what served his agenda or what kind of mood he was in. One of Colt's greatest frustrations was trying to figure out how to deal with Gerry. The mirrors disappeared to be replaced with a blue head with dark eyes. It was Gerry smiling. It was the smile of a trickster. It was the smile of deceit. Colt was relieved when he woke up. He knew that the situation with his boss would not go away, but he didn't want to think about it anymore.

~~~

As usual, Gerry Lathrop's office was organized. Only required items were to be seen and nothing was out of place. However, Colt sensed something much different in the invisible aura of the room. It was as if the office was a façade to hide a much different reality. Shifting waves and crosscurrents of thoughts and emotions littered the psychic landscape of the office. Colt knew that Gerry, the trickster, was adept at hiding his real intent. His inner and outer selves were like two strangers living in the same apartment. One was sane, organized and efficient. The other was egoistic, mercurial, petty and prone to outbursts of jealousy. Gerry entered the room and sat behind his desk. *Now, he's in his power spot. Here it comes. Grrrrr.*

Gerry smiled. It was a short smile; one that could indicate anything. Colt smiled back but felt queasy in his gut. *Why do I feel like I'm about to be kicked by a smiling elephant?*

"Hi Colt. How are things going for you?" asked Gerry

"Okay, I guess," said Colt

I better watch out here, thought Colt. *This guy is hiding something.*

"I just thought it would be good to look over your progress with the job. How do you feel you are performing?" said Gerry

"I'm doing fine," said Colt not wanting to fall into a trap.

"Have you had any problems? Anything we need to discuss?"

"Just the usual stuff," answered Colt.

"A few things have been brought to my attention," said Gerry

Colt could sense a shift in the mood and tried to attune himself to the whole Gerry Lathrop, the sane and the insane.

"I'm told that you're getting behind on your tickets again. Why is that? I thought you were really good at solving Windows problems?" asked Gerry.

"I finish way more tickets than anyone else. It's just that there are so many of them," said Colt

"And there have been the complaints."

"What complaints? I haven't heard of any complaints."

"Two students said you walked out without fixing all of their computer problems."

"Were they girls?" glared Colt.

Gerry seemed to take offense at Colt's attitude. He pursed his lips and shook his head silently.

"It was two girls but that does not matter. You have to do a better job. You can't just leave anytime you feel like it," sneered Gerry.

Colt did not think but reacted like a cornered animal.

"Screw that! One of those girls had her tits all over me and the other asked me if I liked her bra. I don't mess around with customers."

"But, but….," said Gerry

"And another thing. I don't see your UNIX guys doing half as many tickets as I do. It looks to me like you take care of them and leave me to hang in the wind."

"Now, you listen to me. I won't be talked to like that." screamed Gerry, whose entire body was tense. His face was beet red.

Colt stood up and stared at Gerry Lathrop with a clenched jaw and brilliant, angry eyes.

"Do the damn tickets yourself. I'm outta here. Later" yelled Colt.

"Don't come back here," screamed Gerry.

But, Colt was gone.

Colt wandered around the campus contemplating his future. It took him some time to cool off but when he did, he saw that the exchange with Gerry was not handled well. *I lost that one. Even if I was right, I got pissed off when I should have just shut up. I guess I better figure out a plan.*

Chapter 13

Hi Mr. Carbon
Now that I have been working tickets for awhile I see that the PC stuff isn't too hard. But I still don't know a lot about the network here. What should I do?

Colt

------Email-------

Matthew Carbon sat back in his overstuffed chair looking at Colt O'Brien. As usual when not working, he wore jeans and a t-shirt. His kind, perceptive eyes reminded Colt of cold blue water. They were sitting in the front room of the Carbon house. Antique furniture, pictures and other interesting items surrounded them. Colt thought he smelled a faint trace of incense. Many other students had sat in the very same spot that Colt filled at this moment. However, Matthew knew that few had the potential of the intense, dark-haired student who sat facing him. Matthew wanted to help Colt. The young college student had shown great courage and perseverance in the face of overwhelming challenges. Also, Colt displayed the characteristic that Matthew Carbon valued most. He worked hard and did not stop until the job was complete. Matthew saw that the young man was frustrated and wanted guidance. He hoped to be able to give him ideas that would be useful.

Colt was beginning to feel somewhat relaxed as the aura of the room recharged his inner batteries. It was raining outside adding to the cozy, otherworldly feeling of the room. As he always did, he looked up at the ceiling which was painted with wispy clouds. Colt soaked in the ambiance and tried to relax. He did not to plow through the list of problems in his head, until he was able to focus on the answers with an open mind. However, one thing was missing. *I wish Mrs. Carbon was here. There is something about her. She knows what I am going through, at least the psychic stuff.* It seemed to Colt that his experience with Mrs. Carbon had been like an incomplete song. The music was there between them, even when they were not near each other. However, there were few words. They had never openly discussed the varied psychic experiences and dreams that Colt wondered about. That world remained a mystery to him. Strange things happened but did not make sense. Now, he knew that it was not something that would go away after a little while. He would have to deal with it. *She's the one who knows about this stuff. I guess she will talk to me about it when it's time. But when will that be? Crap, why do I have to deal with that dream stuff along with everything else?*

Matthew Carbon looked up, smiled and spoke.

"Well, Colt. I guess it's all coming at you pretty fast? Tell me about it."

"I've got school work, a girlfriend, a tough job and other stuff. It feels like it is one thing after another with no break," said Colt

"Your note mentioned the job aspect. Maybe we should focus on that?" said Matthew.

"Yeah, you're probably right. There's way too much stuff to deal with for one meeting. I had two main things I am worried about. I don't know that much about the network part of my job. Also, I'm not getting any training from those UNIX guys. I thought there would be some Windows guys there too. But I haven't seen any yet."

"What about the politics?"

Colt thought about his blowup with Gerry and the two girls who complained. He knew that he didn't react well to the situation. He even tried playing some rec soccer to cool off. But he knew if he kept at it his interest in computing would fade fast. And, he wasn't about to quit without achieving his goals or at least trying to.

"I guess I am so used to Gerry and his guys playing mind games that I don't think about it much anymore. We had a big fight the other day. I had to call and apologize," said Colt,

"Well, I think I can help with your questions. But, I worry about you having enough time. And, you need to find a way to get along with your boss. The main thing is that you keep your grades up."

Colt thought about everything he was doing to keep up with school and work. Although he considered this a business meeting, he couldn't help thinking about Amy. *Geez. Will we ever have the time or the place to have sex? I sure didn't think having a girlfriend would be like this.* With great effort, Colt pulled his wandering thoughts back to the task at hand. Since his life was full of various forms of work, Colt expected that Mr. Carbon would be suggesting more things to add to his list. Although that might seem daunting for many 19 year olds, Colt was happy to have someone who wanted to help. After dealing with Gerry, it was a huge relief just to have an adult that did what he was supposed to do. The intelligent straightforward man sitting across from him represented hope. Colt became imbued with a sense of optimism. He stopped worrying about what was ahead.

"Please tell me what I have to do. I will try to fit it in," said Colt.

"Okay Colt. Number one is to forget about those UNIX guys training you on anything," said Matthew.

"Why is that?"

"They don't want to deal with fixing PCs. They only want to work on the network and UNIX servers."

"Okay, I guess I knew that they wouldn't help me much. But if they don't want to do the Windows tickets why do they keep making my life so hard?"

"It's arrogance. They can't help it. They think they are so much better than you. So, they make it a self-fulfilling prophesy by screwing with you. When you fail they feel superior.

"What should I do?"

For the next forty minutes Matthew outlined a plan to deal with Colt's job situation. As he talked, Colt thought about how he would juggle the tasks laid before him with his other responsibilities. He could see that in the short term it would be an intense schedule. But his newfound optimism and clear understanding of the steps needed, made him confident that it would all work out.

"Remember, take the Networking Essentials exam to learn about the network. Your network runs TCP/IP protocol. So, it is the same as most Windows networks. There is an exam for TCP/IP but it's also covered in the Networking Essentials material. So that should be enough for now," said Matthew.

"What about the politics while I'm learning?" said Colt.

"I think you should get sick," said Matthew.

"Why would I do that? When I got back there would be piles of tickets," asked Colt

"Let's see how they do without their Windows technologist on the job. If they want to screw with you then let them feel the pain of not having you around for awhile. Also, you can use the extra time to study for the test."

"Well, I remember that exam I took like it was yesterday. I was in such bad shape then. This time it should be easy," said Colt.

"You do the studying. If you need Billy to help you we can set something up. He has helped many students study for that exam. He knows the material better than I do. Then, when you're ready, we'll do the assessment."

Colt smiled and his eyes reflected a newfound understanding as he mulled over what Mr. Carbon said. Having a step by step plan made him feel like he was standing on solid ground. Also he felt confident that he would learn how to deal with Gerry. *So this is politics. I guess there was no way to avoid it. Well at least I have a clue about what to do now.*

Chapter 14

------**Email**-------
From: Sims, Tasha[TSims@wwu.edu]
To: Alioto, Megan[MAlioto@wwwu.edu]
Subject: Big boy bobby

Hey girl
I know hes a freshman but I have my eye on Bobby Jones.
Have you seen him? All tall and handsome. And sooooo
innocent. I think I know how to loosen him up.

Tash

------**Email**-------

Colt sat in his tiny dorm room in the middle of a stack of boxes. He stared out of a window into the darkness. His roommate, best friend Bobby, was absent and missed. *I am soooo sick of boxes in the way of everything. And most of it is his crap.* After looking around the matchbox-sized residence, Colt located his cell phone and dialed. The first thing he heard on the other end of the line was loud voices and music. He could barely make out what Bobby was saying.

"Yah" yelled Bobby.

"Hey, dude. Where are you?" asked Colt.

"Hi Colt. This is a party I'm at."

Sirens started clanging in Colt's head. He sensed that Bobby was in danger and saw waves of red and black emotions surrounding his inebriated friend.

"So Bobby, how did you end up at a party?"

"Oh, yeah, uh, this nice girl asked me to come. She gave me some beers," slurred Bobby.

"So dude, you sound drunk. Is everything okay?"

"Yah, Tasha here said I need to loooosssseen up."

"Where are you?"

"Some house somewhere, lots of people here. Here's Tasha," said Bobby

"Hi Colt. This is Tasha. Bobby came with me. We're at a keg party in a house at 3014 Oak St. He's funny when he drinks some beers."

"Thanks Tasha. Maybe I'll drop by. See you in a bit," said Colt

Although Colt knew that his friend was partying, hearing him in that condition affected him. Bobby had managed to avoid Colt when he had been drinking and it now seemed like a shift had taken place. The reality of a drunken Bobby made the situation more real to Colt; and more alarming.

After looking up the address on the internet, Colt hopped into his purple VW bug and drove to the party. He noticed numerous students of various ages milling outside. Loud music and voices blared out of the two story house. One boy was lying on the grass in the front yard. Two girls looked down at him but did not seem concerned. Colt sat in his car looking at the house. His inner sense told him that the party was in full swing with alcohol as the primary fuel. *Man, I can feel some drunken vibes rumbling out of there. It's like a herd of stupid cattle bumping into each other to get a bite of grass.*

Colt's train of thought was interrupted by a tall girl, with short brown hair, stumbling out of the front door. She took a long step but missed the first stair and fell forward on top of a shorter boy, below. Both collapsed in a heap. The girl sat on the ground in a drunken stupor but the dark haired boy jumped up with both of his hands clenched into fists. His face was red with anger. Colt could see a faint, vaporous, psychic cloud surrounding the menacing student. It was red with dark splotches of black. *Uh oh. I better check this out.*

Colt yanked opened the car door and sprinted across the lawn. When he reached the girl and boy, the irate boy had pulled back his arm to swing at the drunken girl who was in no condition to defend herself.

When he was almost at the two students, Colt yelled "Stop it dude! Stop now!"

The attacker was startled and stopped in mid-swing. Colt grabbed the boy's arm with one hand and his side with the other and yanked hard, twisting him away from the girl. The disheveled boy now stood facing Colt. An uneven blast of hatred hit Colt's inner self like a tidal wave. With his one free arm, the kid swung at Colt who stepped forward, easily avoiding being hit. Now Colt was staring down into the shorter boy's eyes with both of his arms in his solid grasp.

"Dude, do you really want to mess with me?" whispered Colt.

"Uh, er, uh," sputtered the kid

"We both know this can only end badly for you," said Colt.

Courage fueled by anger had now changed into fear. Colt could see the look of a caged animal in the eyes staring back up at him.

"Uh, yeah, I guess I should leave now," he said.

"You do that little dude, you do that," said Colt as he let go with a push.

Colt walked toward the house. At the foot of the stairs, he saw that the girl who had tripped was trying to get up but was unable to. He grabbed her and pulled her to his side. She looked at him with glazed eyes above wobbly legs.

"Hi there. What's your name," asked Colt

"Uh,uh, er…..name?" question the young girl.

"Yeah, your name," questioned Colt

"Annbbbeerr" she said.

"Let's go Amber. Up and in" said Colt

Colt dragged the partier up the stairs. He saw exactly what he expected when entering the house. A mob of young students milled around talking loudly in competition with the blaring music. His inner radar felt an aura of mixed up emotions with a tinge of desire and selfish abandon. *Man, I can do without this. I don't want to be brain dead.* He looked at a nearby group that seemed less intoxicated than Amber.

"Do any of you guys know Amber here," yelled Colt.

A pretty blonde girl answered. "I do. What's wrong with her?"

"She drank too much and tripped. Will you keep an eye on her?"

"Yeah. We're going anyway. We'll take her," said the girl

"Thanks" said Colt as he handed over his drunken package.

Colt looked around the room but did not see Bobby. He walked through the mob toward the back of the house. Beer cans, glasses and, cigarette butts were scattered everywhere he went. The entire house reeked of a mixed of tobacco, rotten food and alcohol. *What a mess. It stinks in here.* Colt looked into the kitchen and saw piles of dishes spilling over the sink. A half-eaten pizza that could have been weeks old lay on a table. Through the noise Colt heard Bobby's voice roaring with laughter. He went into a bedroom and saw Bobby sprawled on an undersized bed in what was obviously a girl's room. Pink flowered wallpaper and various stuffed animals adorned the small room. A short girl with jet black hair was tickling Bobby. She wore worn blue jeans with holes and a flimsy red blouse. She was braless. Both of them seemed to be having a great time.

"Dude. Dude. What's happening?" asked Colt.

The girl looked up with glee emanating from her dancing brown eyes. Brilliant light sparkled from her ears that displayed multiple pieces of embedded jewelry.

"Oh, what have we here? Are you Colt?" she wondered out loud.

"Yeah, I'm Colt. Are you Tasha?"

"I am. I like your friend. He's ticklish."

Tasha tickled Bobby who squirmed with joyful abandon. Colt had seen enough to make him uneasy about the situation. *Crap, he's drunk. This babe is playing with him like a battery operated stuffed animal.*

"Hey Tasha, Bobby and I have something to do," said Colt. Tasha looked at Colt with mock seriousness.

"Wow Colt. It must be really important" she said.

Colt sensed that this playful little girl was not as confident as she pretended. He straightened up standing tall and looked directly into her eyes.

"I see you are having fun but Bobby and I will be leaving now," said Colt.

Tasha cowered slightly under the seriousness emanating from Colt's eyes. Colt grabbed his friend by the arm and pulled him up from the bed.

"Let's go partner. We have stuff to do," said Colt

"Uh, oh, er…whatsss happning, man," slurred Bobby.

"We're leaving dude, hitting the road," said Colt as he tugged Bobby along toward the front of the house.

"Okay, man. Okay. Whatss da hurry?"

As they reached the bottom of the front steps Bobby turned and vomited making loud retching noises as his tall body convulsed.

"That's why dude. Let's go before I really get pissed off."

Chapter 15

------Email-------
From: Carbon, Elyce[ElyceCarbon@AOL.com]
To: Brown, Sasha[Sashabrown2@yahoo.com]
Subject: Family

Hello Sasha

What I meant is that that young man we discussed may not be ready to use his special abilities. You know that it is very tempting to use those powers for the ego and not the better good. It worries me that he is so young and so un-educated in the psychic arts. I asked him to call me if he has any more of those waking dreams. Hopefully he will listen.

E

------Email-------

Colt thought he was dreaming but this wasn't like any dream he had ever had. It was as if he did not have a body and the passing of time was not measurable in any way. He looked at a massive mountain with white snowcaps. It seemed to have rarified air that was clearer than anything he had ever seen. Somehow he knew that there were caves on that mountain where holy men worshipped. With a smooth transition, he found himself in front of a thin, long haired man. The man sat, with eyes closed, in a yoga position. His legs were crossed with arms resting on his thighs. He wore only a wrap that went around his waist leaving his upper torso bare.

As Colt adjusted to his surroundings, he sensed that he was in a cave deep in the entrails of the mountain he had just seen. The man sitting in front of him, though thin, emanated a deep, powerful energy that overpowered Colt, who now felt like a leaf in a constant gust of wind. It was not a physical power but felt like a flowing of invisible energy coming from an unlimited source. And, it was an energy imbued with non-worldly vibrations.

Colt was mesmerized and could only watch and wait as waves of psychic power flowed into him. In a flash the holy man opened his eyes and a silent connection was formed between the two. Colt felt his spine switch on like a soft light bulb. It was as if a pleasant, electrical current was moving through it causing feelings of elation to rise up. Although he could not hear words, Colt knew that the man wanted him to watch and learn. It all seemed so natural in this place. It just was.

After a period of adjustment where both of them became attuned to each other, the unexpected happened. Colt thought the learning would come out of the man but something different happened. A ball of energy formed at the base of his spine. It gained in power as Colt focused on it. Slowly Colt's mind was directed to take that focus and move it up his spine. As he did, it seemed like he found centers that were similar to the ball of energy at the bottom of his spine but with different characteristics. *Each one has its own kind of power*, he thought. *It's like my whole body changes when I get to each one.* Colt felt lighter as his attention moved up his spine. When he neared his head a flash of purplish-white light overpowered him. He started to spin uncontrollably without direction as if in a vortex with no sense of where he was.

As fears rose up, he flailed his arms and legs trying to find his bearings. Suddenly he woke. It took some time for him to adjust to being awake, in his bed, in his dorm room, in Bellingham, in the state of Washington, in the U.S.A. His spine still tingled in multiple spots and his feet didn't seem attached to the ground. *Shit, I better take my time. I've never been that far away or that spaced out. It sure didn't feel like a dream.*

~~~

Elyce Carbon flitted around the house cleaning, straightening and organizing. Since waking in the dark hours of the early morning, she felt a foreboding. She was alone in the house with her thoughts and fears. After eating a late lunch of soup and toast she made herself a pot of peppermint tea and sat in a soft, plush chair in front of the picture window. *I don't need any more coffee. I have to be ready for whatever it is that's coming.* In spite of her desire to be centered and grounded, she felt like the earth was far below her.

Ring! Ring! She was startled by the harsh sounds of the phone. She wondered about letting it ring but was compelled to answer.

"Hello."

"Uh, er, hi. Is this Mrs. Carbon?" asked Colt.

She hesitated while adjusting to the situation. Although she had not been consciously thinking about Colt O'Brien, now it all made sense. The wait was over. He was the reason for her intense feelings of future darkness. Somehow she knew that the future had crashed into the here and now. *He could make a wrong move at any time and create a disaster for himself or others,* she thought.

"Hello Colt. Is everything okay?" asked Elyce.

"Well uh, I remembered that you said I should call if something weird happened. You know, psychic stuff," said Colt.

"Yes, it's very important that you treat those experiences with care," she said.

"Yeah, well I had a sorta dream thing happen," he said.

"Please tell me about it from the beginning. It's very important that you tell me everything that you can remember. Take your time."

Colt was alone in his dorm room. He poured another cup of strong coffee, plopped onto a chair and settled in. *This could take awhile*, he thought. Colt had no difficulty describing his experience with the holy man inside the mountain. It was etched in his mind. Although it was a few days later he still felt the electrical spots on his spine. The entire experience seemed to reverberate through his body and mind. It could have happened minutes ago. When he related what he remembered about, what he thought of as a lesson, he could feel the spinal centers lighting up and energizing him.

"So, it seemed like it was a lesson about these spine things. But it's really weird," said Colt.

Elyce now had a mixture of extreme emotions. She felt relief that she had a clear picture of what was happening with Colt. But, she also knew that he had reached a point of no return. It was a place of danger and instant consequences.

"What's really weird?" she asked.

"Uh, even now when I talk about it, everything seems brighter and I get a really light feeling. It's like a switch got turned on or something. And, I don't know how to turn it off. I think people are noticing that I'm different too."

"Colt, I'm not surprised that you feel this way. It was a lesson and you were switched on. There is so much to tell you that I don't even know where to start," she said.

"Is there something I should do? And, what are those energy things?"

"They are psychic centers along the spine called chakras. Now that you have stimulated them, you will be more aware that they are there.

"Am I okay?"

"I'm going to send you some links to information on this. Most people do not have the same sensitivity that you do. Usually awareness of this comes from yoga and meditation. Because it's very natural for you, it's also very dangerous. I hope we can meet to talk face to face."

"Dangerous? Why?" asked Colt.

"Just think of it as opening a magic box that can't be closed. But, you don't know how to use the magic yet. Please be aware of those centers and the energy and the insights that will come, but don't use the magic until you have more training. That is the danger. Have you ever heard of instant karma?"

"Uh, er, I guess so. It's like payback for doing something," answered Colt.

"Well, for you it means that the consequences of your actions, especially when those chakras are lit up, are very strong and happen very quickly."

"Yeah, no big deal. I'll just watch it and try not to do anything stupid," said Colt.

Elyce cringed at the casual way that he talked. Fears rose up as hidden, future possibilities called to her. As she hung up the phone a sense of dread assailed her. She looked to the clouds on the ceiling of her living room and thought, *I just hope he survives. Oh, how I hope he survives.*

Chapter 16

------Email-------
From: Carbon, Matthew[MatthewC@hocs.biz]
To: O'Brien, Colt[ColtOB@WWU.edu]
Subject: Activity – Field trip

Hey Colt
There will be a job fair at Seattle Center next Friday. We are taking some of the kids to check it out. Why don't you drive down and go with us. It might be interesting.
Matthew

------Email-------

Colt sat between two pimply-faced, 15-year-old nerds in the back seat of a white mini-van. They were talking about how much money they could make doing certain IT tech jobs. The full vehicle and two others, were merging with traffic on highway I-5 going north toward Seattle. Gray skies threatened rain, but had no effect on the bubbling excitement of the high school underclassmen. Colt could sense the anticipation of the students but, was not sure why they were so upbeat. *Why are these little dudes so up about this trip? It's just a job fair. Hell, none of them are old enough to drive, much less get a high-paying tech job.*

The decision to take this trip was easy for Colt. Although a part of him had doubts, he had learned to stick with Mr. Carbon and the certification program. He remembered the last field trip, a visit to Microsoft. It changed his entire outlook on life and spurred him on to success. *No more being stupid for me*, thought Colt. *If Mr. Carbon or his wife suggests something then I'm in.*

After finding a spot in the Seattle Center covered parking garage, the four parents, thirteen young teenagers and Colt met before walking to the Pavilion conference center. They were all well dressed. A few wore ties. One thing which stood out was the baseball style caps that many of the young students wore. Colt knew that Mr. Sweden liked conservative attire. So, he did not wear his usual loud apparel. His attitude toward the program was now the opposite of when he joined as a high school senior. Not only his inner radar but also his experience, told him that only good things would come to him if he behaved. He had reaped the rewards of being a follower, someone who merely heeded the guidance that was provided. He realized how much he was getting in his own way back then. Now he knew better. *Wow, a year ago, I would have laughed at the idea of going anywhere with the little nerds. Now I am wondering what good thing will happen to me.*

Mr. Sweden raised his arm and spoke to the assembled group.

"Let's be sure we always have a parent near each student. Take a look around. Talk to representatives. Let them know about the certifications you've achieved. The idea is to learn whatever you can about getting a job. "

Gunnar Sweden raised his hand.

"What if they think we're too young?" he asked.

"We are not here to prove anything. This is like any other field trip. Learn what you can. There will be plenty of interest because of the certifications you guys have earned," said Ron Sweden.

Mr. Carbon spoke next.

"We will meet at the front door after an hour. It's seven o'clock now so we will meet up eight. We can discuss staying longer then."

The group walked into the large building. Rows of booths with banners lined the huge room. It was close to packed but not shoulder to shoulder. A thin, tall, long-haired man wearing shorts, a T-shirt and tennis shoes approached Billy Carbon. Matthew Carbon stopped with his son.

"Where did you get that hat?" asked the man. "Are you really an MCSE?"

Although the man was not threatening, he startled Billy who was at a loss for words. While he tried to gather his thoughts to answer, a small group of job hunters formed a circle to listen in. Colt could feel a mixture of curiosity, irritation and benign condescension from the assorted group. *This should be interesting. No way these guys can know how smart little Billy Carbon is,* he thought. Finally the high school sophomore answered.

"Uh, yeah I passed the certs," said Billy

"He's passed ten of the exams in all." said Mr. Carbon.

The man stared at Billy in disbelief.

"How did you do that?" he asked.

Matthew Carbon put a gentle hand on his son's shoulder and faced the much taller man and the now even larger circle of computing professionals. He spoke with confidence mixed with a father's pride.

"We have a Microsoft certification program at Highline High School. No student gets a hat unless they earn it. We are here tonight to see what companies think about these students doing the work to get the certifications."

A man dressed in a suit with a noticeably pink shirt chimed in.

"Many of us would love to have an MCSE certificaton. We could put it on our resume. Good luck to you and your students. But they probably won't need it. They have a head start."

"Thanks guys. See you later," said Matthew Carbon.

Colt had been listening and was amazed at how grown computing professionals were taking the young students seriously. By the time the group dissipated, the general vibe from the adults was one of respect if not awe. *I think I'll stick with the Carbons tonight.*

Mr. Carbon, Billy, Colt with a few other students walked together. Many of the booths had tables with company literature and lists of job openings. Smiling representatives talked with prospects or scanned the crowd waiting for qualified individuals to stop by. Colt had no idea what to do, so he observed. He followed along watching , listening and learning. After about ten minutes Billy and Mr. Carbon struck up a conversation with a representative at one of the booths. He looked like he might be from India.

"Hi, my name is Matthew Carbon. The students with me are part of a program we make available to high school students for Microsoft Certification. Can we ask you some questions?"

"Sure. I'm Rahda Singh. As you can see, the need is great for qualified technologists. Tell me about your program."

"Thanks. Could I have my son Billy tell you? He can describe what we do and the certifications our students have."

To Colt's amazement Billy talked to the company representative like they were equals. After about ten minutes, Rahda asked Billy a question.

"Would you like to sit down for an interview with us? Do you have your resume?" asked the friendly man.

"Sure. That would be great," said Billy.

Colt was impressed by two things. First Billy was not in awe but seemed to expect a positive outcome. Second, Billy was prepared. He had a resume and was probably already prepped for an interview. *I forgot how good little Billy is. Man, I still can't*

83

believe he's only a high school sophomore. Every time I see this kid in action, he blows my mind.

As the group walked toward the parking garage, a vision came to Colt. The young students walked through a maze of high cement walls. In a few moments, one by one, they walked through the walls as if they were not there. As he saw them disappear, Colt thought, *Dude, the little nerds don't see any limits. They just go for it.*

Chapter 17

------Email-------
From: O'Brien, Kelly[Kellyobrien@UW.edu]
To: Strong, Amy[AmyStrong@WWU.edu]
Subject: How are you doing?

Hi Amy
I remember when I started college. It was overwhelming. I know when you are an athlete there is that much more to do. And then there is my brother. I love him but he's still a guy. So, if you want to talk let me know. You have my number. Us soccer girls need to stick together.

Kelly

------Email-------

Amy Strong was stewing in a soup of mixed emotions. Feelings of happiness and angst battled to and fro within her young mind. She seemed to have so much of what her heart desired. The transition to school studies and playing on the soccer team had been smooth. Colt loved her and let her know it often. But, as the young school year progressed, an uneasy feeling pervaded her waking moments. She could not explain why this was happening. Unfulfilled desires hovered in the background intruding into her thoughts. Somehow, she thought it would be different. She thought she would be happier.

For Amy, soccer was once the activity that brought the most joy. She had dreamed of mastering the art of passing and scoring and most of all winning. For the most part those goals

85

had been achieved. Now it wasn't enough. Success seemed empty and college had turned into a boring routine. Because of her excellent habits and talent, she was still successful. However, since she had fallen in love with Colt, everything had changed. Now that they were together, she allowed marriage and family to slip into her thoughts with sports and school becoming a distant second. Although she knew that the time line for that step should be years in the future, she was feeling pangs of maternal, nesting desire pulling at her strong sense of purpose. *Why do I want to marry and start a family? It makes no sense. We haven't even finished freshman year. I know Colt isn't thinking about it at all. How am I going to deal with these feelings?*

Amy's cell phone rang softly. She answered
"Hello"

"Hey girl. How are things going?" asked her friend Suzy.

"Hi girlfriend. It's happening again. I feel depressed. " moaned Amy.

"How can you be sad? You have it all, soccer star, boyfriend, good grades. Girls I know are very jealous."

"Oh, I don't know. It's like none of it matters. I have an empty feeling. It's like something is missing. Maybe it's because Colt is so busy with school and working on computers. It's like I never see him. Sometimes I get afraid that he'll just disappear."

"We've been over this. Every girl wants to connect with a guy and have a family. But you have to wait. Both of you have to graduate and get some sort of income," said Suzy

"I know you're right. But, it's like I don't even care. Now that I have Colt, I want to get on with it. It's like if I don't do it now, he could get away. I know it's not very logical."

"Try to hang in there. Give yourself some time. I know a lot of girls that gave in to that desire and ended up with pretty babies but wondered how to pay the bills. And, half of the boyfriends split," warned Suzy.

"Colt would never do that. He loves me," said Amy.

"If you surprised him it might not be the same. And, having a kid is work. I mean it. It's more work than either of us have ever done."

"Oh I wish it wasn't so hard. I don't care about the work or school or any of that." whined Amy.

"Me too girl. Let's get together soon and cry about it," said Suzy.

"I'd like that," smiled Amy.

~~~

Colt was dreaming again. Because of his hectic schedule and lack of sleep, he found it difficult to know the difference between dreaming and reality. Not only was he studying and working on computers, but he was also trying to cram for the Networking Essentials exam. Life was a blur.

The dream had a disjointed quality that made understanding what was happening difficult. He knew that Amy was there. Also, different students he had helped with computer problems came in to and out of view. Gerry, Colt's boss also made a brief appearance. Colt always became suspicious when Garry was around. It did not matter if it was a dream or real life.

Then something odd happened. The confusing images stopped and a feeling of calm came over Colt. It was a delicate, uplifting feeling. Slowly from out of a light purple haze a head emerged. It was a tiny, bald head with fuzzy hair. Two super-bright green eyes pierced Colt's soul. He saw that it was a baby. He felt an overwhelming attraction to the child. The baby seemed more like an angel than a human. It was smiling and appeared to be laughing.

Wow! I never realized how beautiful a baby is, thought Colt. *Why am I seeing this? What is that baby trying to tell me?*

Then Colt thought of Amy and woke with a start. He looked around his dorm room but it didn't seem the same. Colt felt different than he ever had before. He sensed deep down that this dream was important. He could feel it rapidly forming into something concrete. Then it came to him like a lightning bolt from above. Colt tried to tell himself that his conclusions were wrong but knew that there could be only one answer. *Amy wants a baby.*

Chapter 18

------Email-------
From: Strong, Amy[AmyStrong@WWU.edu]
To: Bower, Suzy[susybower@EWU.edu]
Subject: What happened to Bobby?

Susy
I can't believe how Bobby Jones has changed. Mr. Straight and narrow has turned into a party boy. If he is still around after first quarter, I will be totally amazed.
Even Colt is worried about him. I am too.

Amy

------Email-------

The cramped dorm room, with its two simple cot-like beds, was a stinking mess. There was not enough space to be a little bit disorganized and chaos was rampant. Books, clothes, old food and empty beer bottles littered the tiny area. It smelled like stale pizza and beer mixed with unwashed clothes. The stagnant, odorous air permeated the room like a cloud of industrial waste.

It was around twelve o'clock in the afternoon. Rays of sunlight peeked through a slit in heavy floor-to-ceiling drapes. Bobby Jones slept on a bed that was a bit short for his six foot four inch frame. He was dead to the world and snored like he might never wake up. Two beer bottles lay at his feet. On the floor next to the bed a skinny twenty-something girl with red and purple hair, woke with a start, as a patch of light found her face. She wore underwear, a dirty pink T-shirt and multiple tattoos. Her dark makeup was blotched, runny and smeared. The sun reflected as it struck multiple ear and nose rings. She looked around the room for a few moments through, sleepy, world-weary, eyes. After a glance at Bobby, her eyes closed as if she was trying to remember something. She smiled, took a sip from a half-full beer bottle, and kissed Bobby on the forehead gently. After locating the rest of her clothes she got dressed and walked toward the door. As she reached for the knob, the door opened. The startled girl looked at Colt O'Brien. His curt smile belied inner irritation as reflected in his piercing, dark-blue, eyes. The girl was stopped in her tracks by Colt's stare. Since he stood in the doorway, she hesitated, hoping he would move. When he took one step inside, she nodded and scurried past him to the safety of the hall.

Colt stopped abruptly after entering the tiny dorm room. *Ahhh, what's that smell?* He stepped back into the hall leaving the door open. *Crap, I leave for a few days and I come back to a stinky dead-rat dorm room. No way Bobby did this all himself. He must have had a party. I guess it's time to talk to lover boy.* With urgency, Colt sped in and across to the curtains. When he yanked, the curtains flew open allowing a blast of sunlight to enter. After pushing out two windows he turned to look at Bobby who remained in a deep sleep. *I hate this place when it's messy like this. I won't be able to hear myself think until this is cleaned up. And that smell. Aahhhh!*

Colt looked around in the tiny kitchen area for any cleaners he could find. He felt fortunate that there was a half-full spray bottle of 409 and some dishwashing soap under the sink. After starting a pot of coffee he pulled a clothes hamper from a closet and placed it in the center of the room. Then, he placed a kitchen trash receptacle with a new bag next to it.

Bobby was now awake. He looked over at Colt and said, "Hey man, where's Gemma."

"That babe left when I came in. What rock did she crawl out from under?"

"Uh she's ok. She just looks a little weird. We had a great time last night," said Bobby with a wink.

Colt stared at Bobby who now noticed that he was not in a good mood.

"Any girl who could sleep in this pig sty can't be okay." said Colt.

Bobby was now hoping that he would be alive at the end of the day. He was also a bit hung over, which didn't help.

"Uh, yeah. I guess it's a little messy," said Bobby.

"Okay Dude. Here's the deal. I can't wait for you to wake up and help me clean this pig hole. Just stay the hell out of my way. You really don't want to talk to me now. You really don't," snarled Colt.

"Er, uh, okay man," answered Bobby

Colt took one last scan of the entire room and kitchen area and began.

After about forty minutes the clothes hamper was overflowing and two tied trash bags sat by the door. Colt sniffed and searched until he found an open bag with a hamburger and onion rings under Bobby's bed. The odor was overwhelming. *I am afraid to touch it. It's like a disease,* thought Colt. Finally, he forced himself to grab the offending, rotten food using a paper towel and dropped it into a trash bag. Next he grabbed the bag with the two other trash bags and scurried out leaving the door wide open.

Bobby looked around the room which was now neat and clean. Although his head ached, the fresh air and coffee had left him wide awake. After seeing Colt transform the room into something livable, he was ashamed and worried. He looked in the mini-fridge and found two bottles of water. He elected to have another cup of coffee while he waited for the inevitable.

Bobby now faced his longtime friend who was now emotionally composed but serious. He waited to be blasted.

"Pretty bad, huh?" asked Bobby

Colt looked at his deflated, hung-over roommate. He spoke without raising his voice or berating.

"Dude, what's happened to you? I remember when you watched out for me. I was the wild one. Now you don't study. You're on the booze train half the time and you are with a different girl every time I see you."

"Hey man, I'm okay. I just like to have a beer once in a while and hang with chicks."

"Dude, this me. Don't give me that crap. When was the last time you cracked a book. How many times have you woken up and not remembered where you were the night before?"

"Yeah I guess I am partying a little bit. I wasn't trying to have a party here. It just sorta happened," said Bobby.

"Here's the deal. If you don't change now, you will be out of school soon. None of those people at those parties will give a shit either. You don't have any time left."

"Okay Colt. I hear what you're saying."

"And, don't let this place get this bad again. If you do, I will really be pissed off."

"I understand, Colt."

"I have to get outta here before I think about how smelly this place was before I cleaned it up. Later."

The door shut quietly behind Colt but to Bobby it was like a jailhouse door clanging shut in front of him.

As Colt walked across campus, he sensed that Bobby was near the end of his time at school. He knew that it was already likely that his friend couldn't recover from the direction he had chosen. Colt wanted no part of that lifestyle. Just as he was about to attempt to think about something else a thought came into his mind. *I wonder if his stupidity can get me into trouble somehow. Probably not. Soon he'll be gone anyway.*

Chapter 19

------Email-------
From: Strong, Amy[AmyStrong@WWU.edu]
To: O'Brien, Kelly[Kellyobrien@UW.edu]
Subject: Poor Colt

Hi Kelly

I wonder if Colt is trying to do too much. He is really getting mad about his job. That guy Gerry is riding him too. I'm worried that he will lose his scholarship.

------Email-------

It was late. Colt sat in his dorm room staring at his computer monitor. Strong coffee was brewing with a rich aroma wafting through the air. Bobby was not there, which was becoming the norm rather than the exception. After the fight with Gerry, Colt was in limbo as far as his job. He had apologized just to make sure that he wouldn't get fired immediately but still couldn't see himself work for Gerry for much longer. *Crap, I don't even know if I still want this job even if quitting does mess up my life.* If it wasn't for his scholarship and his reputation, he would have had a hard time continuing. He felt that Gerry was an enemy who would never support him. *What am I in school for if that jerk doesn't want to help me learn and get better? Screw him.* On top of everything, Colt was now entranced by his newfound knowledge of chakras and psychic energy. Everything else, except Amy, seemed less and less important. He didn't understand mystical powers but was unable to get his recent experiences out of his mind. *Man, I have to find out more about this stuff. I can feel those chakra energy things a lot of the time now.*

Elyce Carbon had sent him some links to web sites. Colt clicked on a few and looked around but nothing seemed to catch his interest. Then he entered in the word 'chakra' into his web browser and over 100,000 hits came back. He looked at the top listings and clicked on a few without much regard for the topics. *Heck, I don't know that much anyway. Maybe I'll get an idea of what to look at.* One listing displayed the words 'Eastern Mystical Realities'. When he clicked on the link, the page that was displayed seemed like a magnet pulling him. He had a sense, deep within, that this was what he was looking for.

The web site had information about the mystical aspects of many eastern religions. It even had references to Christian mystics. The topics included meditation, yoga, famous mystics, Tibetan Buddhism and even Tantric sex. *Oh, there's something on chakras. I better click on that.* After clicking on the link he started reading about chakras and how to activate them. *Man, these guys are talking about years of meditation, special diets and other stuff to open the chakra centers up. I did it in no time with none of that stuff.*

Throughout the paragraphs of interesting information, were warnings about trying to activate the chakras without proper training and guidance. The word kundalini showed up many times in relation to the chakra at the base of the spine. *I don't see how I can screw this stuff up. It's a natural talent with me. I just won't try to do anything stupid.* After about an hour of reading, Colt was starting to feel overloaded with information. He was wondering if he would understand it any better in the future. In spite of the coffee, he was starting to become sleepy and his mind was not functioning smoothly.

Suddenly, an AOL Instant message popped up on his screen. It was from a user called GuruBoy.

The message in the display area was "Do you want to talk about energy centers?"

Colt wondered how this user, who he had never talked to, was able to communicate with him. However, his curiosity about chakras and mysticism plunged him into the conversation.

"Who are you?" he typed.

"I'm someone who knows a lot about eastern techniques. I saw you were online on my site."

"So that's your web site?" asked Colt.

"It's my site but I have help. I have spent years gathering the information."

"Yeah it's interesting stuff. I can do all that chakra stuff without even trying. It's easy for me."

After a pause that seemed like a long time to Colt, GuruBoy responded.

"Are you self-actuating?"

"What's that? I don't know much. I don't think so."

"Would you like to meet? I know a lot about chakras. I can help you use your abilities."

"Sure. I'm at Western in Bellingham, WA."

"That won't work. I'm in Boston. I would really like to hear more about your experiences. How about a phone call?"

"Yeah, sure."

Colt lay in bed trying to get to sleep. *Man, I see this guy on IM and all of a sudden the energy thingys light up and I'm wide awake. I wonder what he can tell me about all this stuff. Hmmmm, maybe a lot. His site sure has a lot of crap on it.*

The word kundalini came into Colt's head. He sensed that it was a powerful word, even though Colt didn't know what it meant. He said kundalini to himself and in an instant he felt a powerful ball of energy form in at the base of his spine. As he focused on it Colt became light headed. Although he was a bit disoriented, feelings of power and strength came to him. It was as if a solid electrical current was running throughout his body and into the room. *Man, I feel like nothing can touch me. It's like I'm in a bubble of energy that protects me.* After basking in the glow of chakra energy for some time, Colt finally dozed off. Sunrise was a few hours away but Colt would sleep well into the afternoon. His dreams were bright, saturated with color and full of confidence.

Chapter 20

------Email-------
From: Carbon, Billy[billgee@hocs.biz]
To: O'Brien, Colt[ColtOB@WWU.edu]
Subject: Checking in

Hey Colt
Just wondering how the college thing is going for you. I hope to be in
Running Start in my junior year. Maybe I can get some of that college stuff
done early. How is it with fixing computers? Seems like it would be a lot
of work on top of studying.
Billy

------Email-------

Colt was sitting at a computer monitor, working a trouble
ticket, in a cluttered dorm room. As was usual lately, his chakra
centers were humming with mild electrical energy. He found
that whenever he focused his thoughts on a specific thing, this
happened. As his focus increased, the energy he felt did as well.
He felt like he was two people solving whatever problem he was
dealing with. As long as the centers on his spine were lit up,
hidden knowledge seemed to come to him from out of nowhere.
He could solve most of the problems he encountered without
this added boost, but when he felt lost, somehow an idea would
come to him. This had happened enough times that Colt now
depended on this new way of sensing things. The number of
trouble tickets he finished was rising. He didn't know how it
happened. Nor did he care. *This is awesome. I can get an idea of*

what to look at, without doing a lot of research. And, I feel energized all over too.

Back in the here and now, Colt took his time investigating various aspects of the computer. He had already run a diagnostics program that looked at the hardware of the machine. It checked out okay. Now he was finding numerous other problems, including viruses, spyware and unneeded programs running. *This is a mess. I wish I could just format the whole thing and start over. Since I'm going to be here for awhile I might as well relax.* With chakras humming, he settled in for an extended stay.

Colt had not noticed the thin, pimply-faced girl, named Casey, much when he walked in the door. The room was so cluttered that he didn't want to find out about someone who could live in it. And her short, curly brown hair seemed to point in all directions which gave him a feeling that she was a bit crazy or at least eccentric. In the beginning, he had wanted to get the problem fixed and get out. Now he knew it would take some time to fix. After telling Casey that the computer had many problems, he attacked each issue while trying to ignore the claustrophobic atmosphere.

After about fifteen minutes Colt noticed that the girl was flitting around the room like a butterfly. He felt bombarded by thin, streaky, electrical impulses that disrupted his even-flowing chakra energy. He was now finding it very difficult to concentrate in a room full of static that seemed to be coming at him from all sides. *Crap, what is up with this chick. It's like getting hit with electrical popcorn.* Casey interrupted Colt's thoughts. She stuck her head between the computer monitor and his face. A startled Colt clenched his teeth trying not to lash out.

"Uh, er, hi. It's Colt isn't it?" she asked.

Colt pushed his chair back and sat staring at her for a few seconds. *This girl is starting to piss me off. I better watch out. And she better watch out.*

"Uh, yeah," Colt replied.

Casey started peppering him with questions like a machine gun firing at an enemy.

"How long is this going to take? Is my email okay? How bad is the stupid thing? Is it really screwed up?" she asked without seeming to want an answer.

Colt felt like the wired girl would explode if he didn't do something.

"Hey Casey. Can you slow down a little? Lighten up," he said.

Casey stopped talking by clamping her lips together. Her lower lip quivered and her gray vacant eyes twitched from side to side.

"Everything will be fine with your computer, but it will take some time. There's a lot of crap on here," continued Colt.

"What do you mean, crap? I didn't put crap on it. Are you any good at this? I thought it would be done by now," spit out Casey.

"Listen, when you go on the internet and use email, all sorts of stuff can end up on your computer. It just happens. Let me fix it and I'll be outta here," said Colt with a hint of irritation.

"Okay," said Casey as she turned away shaking her curly hair.

Although Casey stopped asking questions, Colt could still see that her scattered, impatient mind was churning. Also he sensed that her frustration was building. He gave up on getting himself centered and his chakras humming again. He plunged into the work hoping that the girl would leave him alone.

Colt decided to fix only what was necessary to get the machine running. *No way I'm staying longer than I have to. This chick is nuts*," he thought.

The problem stated in the ticket was "email not working". Colt decided to work on that. After taking a few minutes to regain his focus and build up his internal energy pool, he went to work. It soon became obvious that spyware had affected the email application. After running a spyware scan and eradicating the offending applications, Colt looked through email folders for any irregularities before he closed the ticket.

Suddenly, Colt felt a jolt of electrical current hit his stomach. He thought he had been electrocuted but sensed that it wasn't real electricity. *It's probably some psychic thing. But what?* He couldn't stop the anger that rose up. It was like a match thrown on gasoline. He turned to Casey. She had hate in her eyes. Her bony body was tensed as if it could break like a dry tree branch in a hard wind.

"Fix the fuckin' computer, you stupid ass. Fix it!" she yelled.

Colt felt a ball of energy build quickly in his stomach. At the same time he was able to see an aura surrounding the angry girl. It was splotchy with dark orange and charcoal spots. Without conscious effort Colt felt and saw a surge of energy arch between his body and Casey. All of the orange spots disappeared from her aura and were replaced by scintillating green streaks. The hatred on the girl's face changed to fear as her entire body trembled and her jaw dropped. She pushed her arms out as if to ward off evil spirits and fled from the cluttered room.

What the hell just happened, thought Colt. *I didn't mean to shake her up that much. Well, at least she's off my back.* He finished fixing the computer and left. As he walked to another location on the

101

campus he thought, *I hope she doesn't complain. Crap I don't even know what happened.*

Chapter 21

------Email-------
From: O'Brien, Colt[ColtOB@WWU.edu]
To: Carbon, Matthew[MatthewC@hocs.biz]
Subject: Total Burnout

Hi Mr. Carbon
I think I am almost caught up now with schoolwork and my tech stuff. But man, am I burned out. I am going to take your advice and really chill out during the winter break. Amy and I are going to Long Beach for a few days, too. Being there always makes me relax. I sure need it. Thanks for your advice. This college stuff is way harder than I thought it would be.
Later
Colt

------Email-------

The beige Toyota Corolla entered the I-5 freeway at the SouthCenter shopping mall area of Tukwila. The skies were gray with a mild drizzle falling on the car and the asphalt highway. Colt sat behind the wheel with Amy at his side. Christmas was over and more than a week remained of winter break. They were pointed south toward Olympia where they would then turn west toward the Washington Coast. *This will be awesome, totally awesome. No damn pager to carry and my cell phone turned off. I already like this,* thought Colt.

Amy leaned over and kissed him lightly on his cheek. She really didn't believe that this was happening yet. After dorm living and rarely seeing Colt, she needed time to adjust to having him all to herself. So many thoughts and desires flitted across her nervous mindscape. She so wanted this to be the most precious experience of her life. She needed her deep love and desire for Colt to find a home in his heart.

"Wow, this is great. I'm glad we get to use the beach house at Long Beach. I wasn't sure if my parents were up for this," said Amy.

"Why not? They know I'm the best thing that ever happened to you," kidded Colt.

"I'm a little freaked out."

Colt leaned over and gently grabbed her hand.

"There's nothing to be freaked out about. We're just moving forward. I'm ready," said Colt.

"I just want it to be really, really great. And, then there's the sex part. I know I shouldn't be nervous but I can't help it."

Colt gripped her hand tightly, quickly kissed her on the cheek and let go.

"Just try to relax while I drive. Let's talk about it in a bit. I hate freeway driving, especially in the rain. It will get better after Olympia."

"Okay, Colt."

Colt concentrated on the road while Amy envisioned every possible scenario on the trip. Most of the scenes were failures of one kind or another. The desire to connect with Colt scared her even though there was no logical reason to be afraid. They were together and nothing indicated otherwise. Colt sensed her uneasiness while trying to ignore the urban sprawl along the Freeway. *I guess I better help her to relax. I'm so happy to be getting far away from school and working computer problems that I didn't even think about what this means to her.*

Just south of Olympia, Colt eased on to the Highway 101 exit going west. He soon slipped into a state of relaxation as they entered a forest of trees. It was as if green hands were massaging away stress with each passing mile.

"It's like the city and school don't even exist," said Amy as she also felt the power of the natural surroundings.

"Yeah, I can really tell how much I needed this. So let's talk," said Colt.

Amy grabbed Colt's arm.

"Oh Colt, we can talk later. It's just that this is really different for me," pleaded Amy.

"Uh, okay. Let's just try to enjoy this. We have our rain gear and running shoes. We can take walks or jog by the water. I'm definitely ready for some trashy reading, too. You know, just unwind."

"I'm being too nervous. I know I am," said Amy.

"I know we're still sorta new to this sex stuff. I'll try not to pressure you. If it feels right we'll do it. But you have to tell me if I'm pushing too much. I am human. And I am a guy."

"I am a little nervous but I really want that. We're together and I love you."

Colt smiled and winked at her as he put his hand on her thigh.

"Just don't use me and throw me away. I'm sensitive too." teased Colt.

Amy hit Colt on his arm but couldn't help laughing.

"Oh you."

After stopping for lunch at about halfway to their destination they drove south toward Oregon. Although it was cold outside, the rain had stopped. The bright sun poured down giving them a feeling of optimism and vitality. They enjoyed the slow, pleasant drive south until they reached the turnoff to go north up the peninsula toward Long Beach. With the Pacific Ocean on their left, and their destination near, the enclosed space became filled with anticipation. After passing through the little tourist town, they pulled into a long driveway that pointed toward the ocean.

"Wow, this is great. I can't believe how close it is to the water," said Colt.

"Yeah, I love it every time I come here. Let's put our stuff in the house and take a walk."

The small house was cozy with two small bedrooms and old rustic furniture in the living room which was connected to a tiny kitchen. Colt noticed paperback books, board games and a small TV with a VCR. A large picture window looked out onto the Pacific Ocean. They could hear the constant roar of large waves from beyond rolling dunes and a wide beach. There were large stands of evergreen trees on the sides of the house creating a feeling of privacy and isolation.

As they walked along the beach the ocean with its large crashing waves, constant roar and overall presence, overpowered them. By the time they returned to the little cabin, Amy and Colt were starting to feel that the frenetic, nervous energy was dissipating from them.

"Did you see those squiggly things?" asked Colt.

"Uh, er, uh…I don't think so. What do you mean sweetie?"

"Well, uh in the air. I can see sparkly, squiggly things that seem to pop up and then go away. It reminds me of pouring a glass of ginger ale and the sparkling spray that comes up. But it's everywhere and always happening."

Amy sat by Colt on the hide-a-bed couch and hugged him.

"I don't see anything like that but I sure feel that way. It's like I am being tickled all over by tiny happy faces. I thought it was just because I love you so much."

"Yeah me too. I think it must be some psychic thing. I'll do some research. Since I had that waking dream experience, I feel a lot different and I see a lot different.

"Later, I want you to tell me again about what happened in that little exam room when you took that test. I never quite got the whole story. But not right now."

Amy held Colt tight and pushed him onto his back. She pinned his arms and started to pepper him with kisses. Colt opened his mouth to allow access. Amy pushed her tongue in and they floated away into a loving dream.

~~~

It was Friday and the last day of their trip. After a few days of stormy weather and being indoors much of the time, the sun's morning rays burst through the picture window of the small cabin. The smell of bacon and eggs woke Colt. The first thing he noticed was that Amy was not by his side. He was now accustomed to her being there. The empty spot emphasized how close they had become. *Man, I don't know how I'm going to go back to that dorm room with Bobby. No way I want to.* Colt, who was naked, slipped into sweat pants and a T-shirt. He walked into the front room and squinted. A smile formed on his sleepy face as the sunlight hit his face. The smells of the food and brewing coffee made his stomach growl. After hugging Amy from behind, he plopped on the couch and stared at the rolling sea.

"Man, am I ready for some of that coffee," said Colt.

"It's almost done Colt. Finally the sun came out," said Amy.

"Yeah, this is going to be an awesome day," he answered.

Amy walked over to Colt and put a steaming cup of coffee, with a strong, pungent aroma, in front of him. She went back to cooking after kissing him on the forehead. Colt grabbed the cup and drank. After a few minutes Amy spoke.

"Okay Colt, let's get out and really enjoy this sunshine while we can. No town trips or any of that stuff."

"Fine with me. I only have one thing I really want to do. We haven't had a good run on the beach yet," said Colt.

"Let's check out the sand and water. We can do a run when it's about to get dark," Amy replied.

"Okay, as long as it doesn't start pouring on us first."

After eating, showering and getting dressed, Colt looked out the front window with a restless feeling. Amy came up behind him, lightly grabbing his shoulders. He turned. She embraced him and whispered in his ear.

"I just hope last night was good for you like it was for me?" she asked.

Colt pulled his head back and stared into her eyes.

"It was great. I knew that it would be okay after we relaxed a little."

"I guess I'm not nervous anymore," she said.

"You were just the way I love you," he said as he held her tight.

As they walked toward the beach Colt thought, *I guess I better be sure to use protection. Last night I almost forgot. Man, when she's sweet like this I forget everything.*

After a full day of walking, wading and exploring, they sat in the front room drinking coffee. It was a few hours before sunset.

"Are you too tired to run?" asked Colt.

"Oh, I'm tired but I need to run. I'm getting out of shape after all those Christmas cookies I ate," said Amy.

"Okay, let's do it. Just tell me if you get too tired," said Colt.

Amy hit him on the shoulder.

"Probably, you will be yelling at me to slow down," she kidded.

The run started slowly as both of them warmed up. Colt stretched and shadow-boxed as he trotted while Amy nodded her head from left to right to stretch neck muscles. After ten minutes they increased the pace but kept together. A pleasant orange-green sunset was beginning to develop creating a feeling of natural ambiance. As both began to breathe heavily, Amy slowed to a fast walk.

"Let's turn around and run hard all the way back," she said.

"Sounds good to me," said Colt.

By time they got to the little cabin Colt and Amy were physically spent. Both felt exhilarated in spite of sore muscles. Before they knew it darkness had set in. After a quick dinner Colt was already becoming sleepy.

"I'm going to shower and get into bed," he said.

"I'll come in later. I'm not quite ready to let go of this last little time we have here."

After a long soothing shower, Colt dried off and practically collapsed into the bed. By the time Amy was finished with her shower, Colt was in a deep sleep as evidenced by an occasional snore. She sat on the porch listening to the pounding surf and soaking in everything. She wanted to remember and take as much of the experience with her as she could.

Although she usually wore pajamas, Amy jumped into the small bed with nothing on. She snuggled up next to Colt. Soon she was also sound asleep and dreaming sweet dreams. It was pitch black when Amy woke. The sounds of the crashing waves soothed her. Her body was a bit sore but it made her feel alive and vital. She was a little warm but turned over and snuggled next to Colt. She noticed that he smelled especially good for some reason. In a short time her loving feelings for Colt became overpowering. *Oh, I love him so much. If I could only just kiss him a little,* she thought. She put a hand on his shoulder and gently started to pull him toward her. Though still more asleep than awake, he finished the rotation into her arms. They kissed for only seconds before they united. Neither of them could resist or wanted to.

Chapter 22

------Email-------
From: Bower, Suzy[susybower@EWU.edu]
To: Strong, Amy[AmyStrong@WWU.edu]
Subject: It's time

Hey girl

I can't wait to hear about your trip. I know we just started school again but we have to get together. No phone stuff. Face to face. Can we meet in Burien soon? I kjust now it was soooo romantic...

SuzyQ

------Email-------

Amy was almost settled in after the trip to the ocean. It took a few weeks for her to recover. The long layoff and the sense of loss at being separated from Colt again had made it difficult to care about school or anything else. Not a minute passed when she didn't think about being with Colt permanently. She wanted to wake up by his side forever.

Everything had changed in those few days together. When they went to their separate dorm rooms, after returning to the campus, she cried for hours. She had tried to hide how strong her feelings were but she knew Colt could feel her emotions like a thick fog filling up the car on the ride home. The entire trip back to school she prayed that he wouldn't mention their last night of lovemaking and the lack of protection. *It was my fault. I screwed up*, she thought.

Amy didn't want to make the two hour drive to Burien to see her best friend Suzy, after settling in to a routine. She had finally gotten to the point where she wasn't feeling crazy all the time. But, she needed to talk to someone. Suzy was the only one that she felt close enough to and trusted. Although she was functioning at school, her dream of living with Colt would not go away. Their living situation was not helping. It seemed that it was either all or nothing. And, at school with all of their separate activities, it was nothing. She rarely saw Colt and when she did it was with others. She ached to be with him alone. She craved exclusive access. *I need to see Suzy or I will go totally bonkers. Ahhhh!*

It was still cold and rainy in Burien as the new year slowly inched forward toward spring. Amy, who was bundled up, walked into the Burien Starbucks. A green, knitted wool cap covered her head and accented a deep brown jacket. She saw her friend Suzy sitting at a corner table and smiled. Two tall cups already were on the small table. Suzy noticed that it was not a smile of abandon but one with reservations.

"Are you okay," asked Suzy as Amy removed her coat and cap.

Amy cringed a bit and sat down. Her eyes were focused on something other than her friend as thoughts overwhelmed her.

"Uh, is it that obvious?" she asked.

"Well yeah. You look like a deer in the headlights girlfriend. Tell me all about it. I think I already know anyway," answered Suzy.

"Well, the trip was great. I just love him so much. And now, it's like I never see him at all," said Amy.

"Tell me everything from the beginning. God I wish I had a boyfriend. I meet lots of guys that want to sleep with me but not much else. It's really frustrating. You don't know how lucky you are," said Suzy.

Amy related the events of their trip. She left nothing out but skipped the intimate details. A romantic glow grew, the longer she talked. She realized that it was probably the highlight of her life, so far. As she neared the end, she remembered their last intimate encountered and guilt overcame her.

"Okay, Amy. I think I get the picture. But what happened at the end. It sounded like heaven but I saw that look," asked Suzy.

"Uh, er, I sorta screwed up. Colt's not mad or anything but I'm mad at myself,"

"Let's see. What could you have done? Hmmmm?" asked Suzy with a knowing tone.

Amy stared at her as tears formed in her eyes. Her face became pale. A look of understanding came to Suzy. She put her hand on Amy's shoulder.

"Oh Amy. You're not the first girl to forget to take precautions in the middle of being in love. If that's what it is, just forget about it and move on. You know the odds," said Suzy.

"I know it happens but the thing is, I just don't care. I want us to be together. I want to have babies. I want to start a life," said Amy.

Suzy thought about her friend's situation and envied her. She knew the timeline for everything was messed up by Amy's feelings, but still she wanted to have that kind of love for someone. Suzy tried to think of what to say. Both girls sat in silence sipping their coffee drinks. Finally Suzy broke the silence.

"Listen girl. You have what we all want. You love him and he loves you back. But, you have other stuff to do, don't you?

School, soccer, being young and free. Once you move on to the next thing some stuff will never have a chance of happening again."

"I know all that but I don't care when I think about him. It's like I get really stupid about all the stuff I should be doing. What am I going to do? And, I worry too. There are pretty girls all over the place. And I know there are plenty that would take him away from me with no guilt at all."

"Have you talked to Colt about how you feel?" asked Suzy.

"Not really. I think he knows I love him a lot but that's it. I haven't mentioned the M word."

"All I can say is that you have to try to hang in there. Maybe you guys can move in together in a year or two. But don't get so caught up in things that you forget about taking precautions. And, he needs to watch it too. Maybe what happened is like a warning. Life is telling you to watch out or you'll have big decisions to make."

"Yeah, I'll try. But it's really, really hard."

Chapter 23

From: O'Brien, Colt[ColtOB@WWU.edu]
To: Carbon, Billy[billgee@hocs.biz]
Subject: The test

Hey Billy

I'm about to study for the networking essentials test. I have a few books and the practice exams. Is that enough? I can use all the help you can give me. Im overloaded as it is.

Colt

------Email-------

With Colt's busy schedule he was forced to set aside time to study for the Networking Essentials exam. He knew that it would be difficult. but by cutting corners on his school study and his job, he was just able to allot an hour a day to pore over the material. He spent more time on the weekend. This schedule cut even more into the time he could spend with Amy. When he studied for the first exam, she was at his side giving him support. This time, it was almost impossible for Amy to study with him. Colt knew that she felt left out, but he felt that having her involved for only a small part of the time he needed, would be like a tease. He hoped to pay her back later on.

Colt had studies for a week of study and was beginning to feel confident that he was starting to understand the material. After a slow start due to boredom and the necessity of learning the meaning of new words, he started to gain momentum. The

115

primary motivator for him was that his learning related directly to his job fixing computers that were attached to the school network. He also saw that this was the logical next step in his learning. He could see that once he mastered this material, new opportunities would be available to him. Also, he remembered many times when other technologists would use words like 'TCP/IP', 'router', and 'protocol' leaving him bewildered. Now the meaning of those words was becoming clear, which gave him confidence.

Toward the end of the second week of study, Colt followed Mr. Carbon's advice. He hoped to take the exam on the next Sunday but needed a few days to cram. He sent an email to Gerry on Thursday morning saying he wasn't feeling well and would be out sick. He knew all of the trouble tickets would sit until he returned anyway. So, he didn't feel any guilt about fibbing about his health. He hoped that he would be missed, however. *I'll just be busier when I get back but maybe Gerry will start to see that he needs me.* To be gone any longer would be too painful for him and his customers. He made arrangements to obtain notes for classes he would miss. When he had everything organized so that he could focus only on studying for the exam, he called Amy.

"Hi," said Colt.

"Uh, hi. Wow, you surprised me. I thought you were in a black hole and you might never come out," she teased.

"Listen I called in sick and am going to miss classes for the next two days. Maybe we can get together tomorrow," said Colt

"And do what?" asked Amy who was now curious.

"Well, I think I can kick out Bobby and you could help me study like we did for the first exam. You can ask me all the questions."

Amy almost cried as she relived the experience of working with Colt on the test. It was when they first truly connected. Her eyes started to glisten.

"I'd really like that," she said.

Colt crammed all day Thursday. In the afternoon he focused on practice exams that were on his computer. By the end of the day he felt confident that he could pass the real exam. At about 9 am the next morning a knock came on Colt's door. When he answered, Amy walked in with a large pouring container of Starbucks coffee and cinnamon rolls that were still warm. She set down the offerings on the small table. Colt grabbed her and held her tight. Amy responded by swaying slightly. She whispered in his ear.

"I was going to wait until we had coffee but I want you now."

She then pushed him onto the bed and proceeded to pepper his face with delicate kisses. Colt couldn't help himself.

"Oh, oh, don't you want to study with me?" he teased.

She started to pull up on his T-shirt.

"I'll teach you a thing or two, Colt O'Brien."

"Uh, okay. Just asking," said Colt allowing Amy to do as she pleased.

~~~

It was Saturday, the day before the Networking Essentials exam. From the street Amy and Colt looked up at the Carbon home. The house was a light shade of purple and seemed to glow in the bright sun. It was cool but the air was fresh. Everything was still wet from the recent rain.

"Wow, what a color. I've always wanted to see what this place was like inside," said Amy.

Once in the house, both Colt and Amy, who were sitting on a soft couch, absorbed the delicate ambiance of the living room. As usual, Colt became deeply relaxed. It was as if his body, mind and soul were all being massaged. *I better put on my thinking cap for this assessment,* he thought. Matthew Carbon sat in one chair looking at Colt and Billy Carbon sat in another next to him. A pile of books and sheets of papers were stacked in front of them on a folding table.

"So, you've been through this assessment before. Billy will pick anything he wants and drill you on it. At the end we'll give you the go or no go verdict," said Mr. Matthew.

"You have a beautiful house. I just love it," said Amy.

"That's because of my wife. I'll pass along what you said. She's not here right now," answered Matthew.

Billy looked at Colt and smiled. The young teenager seemed ill-suited to the role of assessor, if for no other reason than he looked so young. *I wonder if Billy has ever kissed a girl,* thought Colt. Although it was difficult to see beyond appearances, Colt knew that a vast store of knowledge was inside the young man's head. And most of all, it was organzied.

There was a stack of books and papers as reference material but Billy started without using any of them. He asked Colt simple questions which he immediately answered correctly. After about fifteen minutes, Billy spoke.

"You seem to know this stuff pretty well. I guess you really studied."

"Yeah, when you get into college you learn to study or die. So, I had to get better," answered Colt.

"Uh, yeah. Let's move on to protocol stuff," said Billy.

After another half hour of more difficult questions that came straight out of Billy's head and a few practice questions that he read from sheets of paper, Billy turned to his dad.

"He's ready," he said.

"Okay Colt, you passed. Billy, give him a few really difficult questions before we end this thing," said Matthew.

Billy asked Colt a question that involved a mixed network with UNIX, Windows and Apple computers using the TCP/IP protocol. The question dealt with what pieces of hardware and software were required for all of the devices to communicate with each other. Colt thought about it for a few minutes as Amy looked at young Billy in disbelief.

"Uh, little dude. No way I'm ready to answer that one," said Colt.

"I just had to let Billy show off a little. Most people have no idea of his abilities. We are working on getting him a teaching job. Pretty good for a high school sophomore, huh?" said the proud father.

"He's so young that it's easy to forget how smart he is. Until he starts with the questions, that is. I'm a believer," answered Colt.

"We'll see you guys tomorrow at the testing center. It's at one, right?

"Yeah, I think it should be no problem. See you then," said Colt.

~~~

Colt was very confident and didn't want to do any studying on the day of the exam. However Amy had insisted that they arrive 40 minutes early and that he do one last scan of the material. Now he found himself in the small testing room, sitting in front of a thin computer monitor. He started the exam and finished the first question with ease. *This will be a piece of cake. Not like last time*, he thought. In spite of his confidence, as he remembered back to the first exam, his stomach tightened up and tremors overcame him. He started to relive that experience with all of its emotional and physical elements. He found himself transported to that time and place. As he floundered helplessly, he struggled to recover his composure and gain solid footing. After some time he stopped fighting the waves of pain that were assailing him. From a center within himself, he waited with no expectations. After what seemed to him to be a long time, he heard music. It started softly but soon became clear. He recognized the song immediately but couldn't remember the name or the group. It was a subtle vibrating song that featured a sitar and muted drums. He heard the words *'Try to realize it's all within yourself - no-one else can make you change. And, to see you're really only very small. And, life flows on within you and without you.'* The song soothed him and when he realized that it was a Beatles song he was hearing, he felt whole again.

Wow, I better get on this test. How long was I screwed up for? Colt looked at the time remaining and saw that he had thirty-nine minutes, of an eighty minute test, left. He focused on the next question and moved forward. The song stayed with him as background music as he moved quickly through the exam. With ten minutes to spare he reviewed the few questions that he had marked and ended the test. He grinned as the green bar flashed on the screen indicating success. Also he noticed that he had a score of 85%.

Colt gave the thumbs up from the top of the stairs. Amy, Mr. Carbon and Billy clapped from below as he hopped down the steps.

Chapter 24

------Email-------
From: O'Brien, Colt[ColtOB@WWU.edu]
To: O'Brien, Leona[LeonaB@aol.com]
Subject: Mrs. Carbon

Hi Mom
On my last trip home I went over to Mr. and Mrs. Carbon's house. Both of them have been very helpful with school and other stuff. You know about the way I dream and see stuff. It's been our thing. Well, it turns out that Mrs. Carbon knows a lot about what I'm going through. That's good because lately I've had a lot happen of the weird variety. So I told her some of it. If you have questions about psychic stuff, she might be a good person to get to know. I know she is helping me deal with stuff. Colt

------Email-------

The drive from Bellingham to Normandy Park allowed Colt to think about the numerous topics on his mind. He needed a break from school, his computer job and Bobby Jones. He was hoping this three-day weekend away from Western would allow him to organize things and come up with some ideas to balance his life. Also, he had not been giving much attention to Amy. She had not said anything but he knew she was feeling left out. *Crap, I've got way too much stuff to deal with. I wonder if I'll get any of it right?*

Large droplets of rain began to spatter against the windshield of Colt's VW as he pulled up in front of his house. It was nearing dinner time and he was ready to get out of the old, run-down, car and eat. His mother met him at the front door. She immediately hugged him like she never wanted to let go.

"Oh honey, I miss you every day you are gone," she said.

"Hi Mom. It's great to be here. I needed a break," said Colt.

"Just relax and forget about all that school and work. If you need anything I'm here. Dinner will be ready in a half hour."

Colt walked to his room to wait for dinner. *Dude, you need this.* He looked out the window at the pouring rain and tried to prioritize his list of things to accomplish. After about five minutes he realized that his mind was overloaded and not working in a rational manner. *Screw this. I'm getting nowhere. I'll figure it out later.*

~~~

Elyce Carbon sat in front of her husband. In spite of her petite stature, she seemed larger than life. Her intense, sea-blue eyes beneath bright red hair, stared directly into those of her husband Matthew. When she was like this he knew to be alert. He knew he would hear her say something serious and important.

"I know that young man, Colt O'Brien is stopping by. I need about ten minutes with him," she said.

"Okay, honey. Is something wrong?" asked Matthew.

"It's a metaphysical thing. He is very sensitive. He can feel things. I need to talk to him about it."

"Alright, you can have him first. Take as much time as you need."

"No, you do your thing with him, first. That is very important, also. This child lives in two places at the same time. I just hope we can help him to deal with it."

At that moment they both saw Colt walk in front of the picture window toward the front door. Elyce slipped away to another room. After settling in, Colt began to relax. The clouds on the ceiling, the ambiance of the living room with its antique furniture, and Mr. Carbon, helped him to release stored up tension. To Colt it all seemed like an emotional massage. He could feel inner batteries recharging. Then, he remembered or rather felt Elyce Carbon. He recalled the out of body experience from another time. He could see her face emanating light as clearly as when it happened. *Wow. I still don't know if that was real or what.*

Matthew Carbon opened the discussion.

"Well, Colt. First of all I want to congratulate you again for passing the Networking Essentials exam. I expect you got behind in your work to study for that."

"Yeah I'm overloaded, but now I understand what networking is. I need to learn more but at least I've started," said Colt.

"The last time we met we formed a plan. It looks like you followed most of it. Did you take some time off from your job like I suggested?"

"Yeah, I told them I was sick. Then I crammed for the test. Even Gerry seemed happy when I started doing tickets again. And he isn't messing with me as much."

"That's great. I think I can guess what you're dealing with now. You tell me the things on your mind and we can sort through them. It's always better to prioritize and then work one thing at a time. I hope that now you will learn that you can't do everything, at least not well."

Colt talked and Matthew Carbon listened. As he talked Colt realized how many things he was dealing with. He discussed Bobby Jones, his networking job, schoolwork and numerous other things. It was as if an ocean of dammed up mental and emotional liquid was slowly being released giving him room to fill the space with new ideas. He could see that he had been juggling too many large balls and was struggling to keep up. When Colt stopped to take a breath, Matthew organized what he had said into a coherent list of broad areas to deal with. He then prioritized the list and gave simple, straightforward advice for each item. One thing that surprised Colt was the suggestion to be sure to do something fun and relaxing on a regular basis. After about an hour and a half, Colt had a plan of attack and having achieved that goal uplifted spirits.

"Remember Colt. The most important thing is to get through the first year of school. Anything associated with that needs to be at the top of the list," said Matthew.

"I see that. It's much clearer now," said Colt.

"Also, I hope that your job will get easier now that they appreciate you more. Since you don't have to study for the Networking Essentials exam, you should have a little more time, too. It's too bad that your scholarship is based on doing that job. I know it puts pressure on you."

"Yeah, I think those guys should be helping me, not making the job harder."

"Life is like that sometimes. Keep Mr. Sweden and I informed through email. We'll give you strategies to deal with anything that comes up. Remember, if you perform, they will not be able to let you go. They won't have anybody else to do the work that they don't want to do," said Matthew

"I will try to follow what you are telling me. Thanks," said Colt.

"Oh, my wife would like to talk to you for a few minutes."

Elyce, who had been listening in silence, stepped forward and sat in her overstuffed, antique chair by the picture window.

Matthew left the two in silence patting Colt on the shoulder as he passed.

"Hello Colt. It's great to see you," said Elyce.

"Hi Mrs. Carbon," said Colt

"I wanted to talk to you about the other things you are experiencing. Those things may seem weird to you."

"Yeah I have funny dreams and sense things. I saw you in a waking dream," said Colt.

"You have special abilities that allow you to see and feel the other side. You have raw psychic talent but there is a price to pay when you make mistakes. You need to learn the correct way to use your powers," said Elyce

"How do I learn that stuff? I don't know if I even want to. I looked some stuff up on the internet but there's a lot out there," said Colt.

"Right now, you must try to let things come to you. You may have a difficult time staying grounded in this reality as you adjust to this new state of consciousness. You may feel, at times, that you are in two places at once."

"Okay, I'll try to let it happen and learn," said Colt.

"If you find yourself in a dream that you can't wake up from, think of me. I'll be watching. If I come to you in a dream, follow me."

"Okay, Mrs. Carbon. Thanks."

"It will take some time for you to find your way. Much of what you need to learn will not be from books or talking. Allow yourself to be guided. If you try to make things happen without being open to guidance, your ego will certainly try to take over. And that can lead to disaster. So, listen, watch and learn. And most of all don't try to force things to happen. Let life unfold without manipulating situations. Goodbye Colt."

"Goodbye Mrs. Carbon," said Colt as he walked out the door.

Chapter 25

------Email-------
From: Carbon, Elyce[ElyceCarbon@AOL.com]
To: Brown, Sasha[Sashabrown2@yahoo.com]
Subject: I see darkness

Hello Sasha

I am sure you remember that young man we discussed with the special abilities. Lately, I have been having dark thoughts about him. It feels like a storm is coming and I don't think he can handle it. I pray that he will survive. Let's talk. He may need our help

Elyce

------Email-------

Colt was floating in darkness. He had difficulty focusing or seeing anything for that matter. The more he tried to find his way and see something, the more he became confused and disoriented. *Will I ever get out of this hole I'm trapped in?* Then as if someone heard his question, the darkness lifted like a thick blanket being pulled back. He stood in a desert surrounded by sand dunes. A giant, white, heatless sun beamed onto him. *What is that? I sense something.* He felt drawn to the top of a nearby dune. He strained to see the source of the pull that was increasing by the second. As he peered at the movement he saw what seemed to be a red swirl. It appeared to be moving toward him. Soon, he was able to make out that it was a large snake. It was side-winding down the dune leaving an ess pattern behind. The scintillating red color was hypnotic and Colt could not divert his gaze away from the slithering reptile. When the creature was close it stopped, and reared up, looking straight at Colt. *What is it about this thing? It seems so different? And why am I not scared?* Then he realized what was odd, what was not snakelike at all. Its eyes were like those of a baby deer. They radiated innocence and need. It was un-threatening to the point of eliciting sympathy from Colt. As Colt tried to move a bit closer, he found that his legs were like cement pillars going deep into the sand. *What the hell?* When he looked up from his buried legs, the snake started to transform. Its light red color darkened as it moved toward him. Colt tried to get away without success. *I don't think I'm going to like this. Aaahhhh.* Now the creature started to grow. It continued to expand until it touched him. It felt hot in an electric sort of way. His entire being started to feel like it was being bombarded with tiny, kinetic, lightning bolts. Now, the crimson reptile was higher than he was tall. Colt could see large glowing scales directly in front of his face. The enormous snake started to roll onto him. Colt felt like he would explode in a blaze of sparks or suffocate under the weight of the creature. He fought with every ounce of energy he had, but was almost submerged. *Ahhh! Ahhh! Help!* He woke in a overheated sweat. The dread and feeling of sparks arcing through his body was still present. He felt like he was trapped halfway between the real world and the dream world. *Crap! That was way too real. I still feel like a little mouse under a big snake. I need to do something to help me forget about that big monster.*

~~~

Colt strolled into his dorm room. His day had been busy but fulfilling. He had attended classes and then worked computer tickets for a few hours. *Nice to get some stuff done,* he thought. He plopped down in a chair and sipped on a large cup that had a Starbucks logo on the side. It was about eight in the evening.

The musical ring of Colt's phone caught his attention.

"Yo, this is Colt."

"Is this Bobby's friend?" said a high pitched, worried voice.

"You mean Bobby Jones?" said Colt

"Yeah, uh huh." said the girl's voice.

"Yeah, he's my roommate. What's up?"

"You better get over here. He's being stupid and he's pissing off some bad dudes."

"Where are you at?"

"The graffiti house. Do you know where it is?" said the voice.

"I'm on my way. Later," answered Colt.

On the short drive to the location, Colt thought about Bobby. *This guy is messing up. And, it's getting old. I can't keep bailing him out of trouble.* As he pondered the situation, a cloud of gloom descended upon Colt. It gave him a feeling of being lost and abandoned. He started to feel that the entire universe had forgotten about him and nobody cared. With great effort, he was able to separate himself from the negative feelings. He treated it like a foreign invader that was trying to assault him. *Where the hell did that come from? Very weird.*

Colt walked toward the open door of the graffiti house. The entire front was spray painted with intricate, multi-colored, day-glo designs and figures. He liked the colors but did not like the style of the art. It seemed gang-like to him. As he reached the front door a feeling of dread came over him. At the same time, he smelled pot smoke from within the house. Colt paused on

129

the porch and tried to get control of his emotions. He wanted to run as far away as fast as possible. *What is it about this place that is making me feel so weird?* After a few minutes the aura of the house, with its intoxicated inhabitants, seemed to have an effect on Colt. In spite of his determination to be alert and responsible, he became somewhat intoxicated and relaxed. His fear slipped away in a haze of contentedness. *Uh, why was I here? Oh yeah, Bobby.* When he walked in, Colt saw Bobby sitting with a girl on a large couch. She wore black with heavy mascara. They were obviously intoxicated. This seemed interesting to Colt. *Uh, Bobby is with a goth chick,* he thought. With each step toward his friend Colt became more relaxed and less focused. The pot smoke or group vibrations were still having a powerful affect on him. Things were becoming colorful and expanding around him with each second, but his ability to think logically and make conscious decisions was becoming diminished.

"Hey Colt, why are you here?" said a laid back Bobby.

"Uh, er, uh. I got a call, I think?" said Colt.

Colt felt a rustling behind him. Through the buffered internal walls in his mind, it was like the furious flutter of butterfly wings in the far distance. When Bobby opened his mouth to speak, Colt was yanked away from the couch. He was in no condition to resist and spun around flipping onto his back. The world was turned upside down but to Colt it was a pleasant, slow-motion movie. He was intrigued but not alarmed. Then, Colt O'Brien's life changed forever.

Chapter 26

------Email-------
From: O'Brien, Kelly[Kellyobrien@UW.edu]
To: Strong, Amy[AmyStrong@WWU.edu]
Subject: This isn't good

Hi Amy
We almost took Colt to the hospital. He's like a zombie. I
wish I could help him. What are we going to do?

Kel

------Email-------

The short fall was like a slow-motion movie but the landing
was a catapult into an extended nightmare. Colt had always
avoided anything resembling drugs. He did not know the exact
reason but he had rarely been around drugs of any kind. When
he breathed in the marijuana smoke in the graffiti house and
became attuned to the vibrations of the partiers, it was the same
as if he had smoked marijuana; a so-called contact high. The
effect was immediate and strong. He lost his drive, focus and
mental clarity as he tumbled into a drug-like stupor. He relaxed
mentally and physically to the point of not being able to
function.

When he was pushed away from Bobby Jones, he did not
and could not resist. His body flew to the side and down onto
the sharp corner of a table. When the tip of his spine hit, it was
like a fast stream of molten lava shooting up his spine to his

head and then erupting. After the eruption, the fire penetrated the rest of his body. The intense pain caused him to breathe in like a swimmer about to be pulled under a powerful wave in a stormy sea. The pain lasted for a few seconds before Colt was taken to another place. It was a place not connected to this earth or his body. The pain was gone but so was Colt.

To the world, Colt looked dead. He lay motionless, on the floor, the smashed table beneath him. It appeared that he was not breathing. Most of the stoned students backed away in fear, wanting nothing to do with a dead student. A few stared at the lifeless body on the floor. After a few seconds of looking, the majority were leaving as fast as possible. Bobby Jones moved toward Colt and leaned over him.

"Oh no! This looks bad, really bad," he whispered to himself.

Then something odd happened. After a night of beers and pot, for some reason Bobby became almost sober. He felt a tingling throughout his body. He sensed that he needed to take his friend back to their dorm room. There was no hesitation. For Bobby, who was looking for guidance, following this strong urge was a way to simplify a crisis situation. He looked up at a tall, skinny student standing by him.

"Hey man, help me get him up. I need to get him back to our room," said Bobby.

"Are you sure? He's in bad shape. Heck, he might even be dead," said the frightened young man.

"Just help me. Just do it," ordered Bobby.

It surprised both of them when Colt was able to halfway stand, as they dragged him out of the house. Colt started mumbling. He was incoherent and his glazed eyes looked to a faraway place that only he could see. They piled him into Bobby's Toyota Corolla and Bobby drove off. Bobby looked at his friend in the seat next to him. Tears were forming in his eyes.

"I'm sorry, man. I'll take care of you," he said.

The next day Colt awoke with a splitting headache. *Oh man, something is wrong with me.* It was about nine on a Friday morning. He tried to sit up but his neck felt like it had been operated on with a huge nutcracker. Along his spine to the top of his head he could feel his chakras. But they seemed much more pronounced than before. When he concentrated on a specific part of his spine, he was pulled into a hallucination of bright geometric figures spinning around.. The base of his spine was throbbing in a different way. It was also emanating pain; a deep, penetrating, debilitating ache. He looked inward to the base of his spine and was transformed to the place he remembered from his dream. The large, crimson, doe-eyed snaked was coiled in front of him. Its eyes penetrated his mind and soul. He could feel it telling him, "You are mine now, you are mine"

"Hey Colt. Are you okay?" asked Bobby Jones

Colt did not respond. Although his eyes were open, he looked like he was hypnotized, to his friend. Bobby stood Colt up and tried to walk him around the dorm room. Colt was like a piece of limp seaweed and could barely stand. He said nothing.

"C'mon Colt, snap out of it. Wake up."

Now the crimson snake was slithering away releasing its grip on Colt. The hallucination vanished being replaced by the cramped dorm room. It was like a door to a dungeon opened and a blast of harsh light assailed him.

"Uh, whaaaa, oh,,ahh. Down, let me down," said Colt

"Man, are you okay? What happened?" said Bobby.

Colt looked at his concerned friend. Everything was bright and dizzying.

"What's the orange glow, Dude? It's all around you," said Colt.

Then, Colt collapsed in a heap.

Chapter 27

------Email-------
From: Jones, Bobby[BJones@WWU.edu]
To: Smith, Todd[Toddsmith3@aol.com]
Subject: My friend Colt

Hey Man
I really really screwed up. What a mess.

BJ

------Email-------

Bobby wasted no time before calling Colt's parents in Normandy Park. Colt was in and out of wakefulness but even when he was conscious he babbled incoherently. Bobby had no idea how to deal with the situation and wanted no part of explaining what happened to school authorities. When he was asked to bring Colt home he felt like a huge dark boulder had been lifted off of his back.

Bobby's worries about his friend only increased as they careened down the I-5 freeway toward Seattle to the south. Although Colt was the one seemingly in trouble, Bobby was overcome with fear for himself. Disgust and guilt were also foremost in his mind. It had been only one day since Bobby was last inebriated but he craved alcohol. Through the ordeal with Colt he had been forced to focus on something other than where the next party was. This resulted in an unusual clarity which had a profound effect on him. *Shit, I guess I've been in a daze. Stupid me. And to think that I felt like I was in control.* To

135

Bobby it was bad that he had lost his moral compass and that his chances of continuing school were bleak. However, the thing that shamed him the most was that his friend was in real trouble because of him. *It's my fault and I can't drink myself into believing anything else.*

The two friends pulled into the O'Brien's driveway in Normandy Park. Colt was slouched in the passenger seat next to Bobby in a semi-conscious state. Colt's mother, father and sister stood, waiting. They all looked like they were attending a funeral. Colt's mother saw her son and started to cry. Even his strong, tall, father cringed with dread. When Colt exited the car of his own volition, everyone was hopeful, Bobby most of all. Colt looked at his family in surprise.

"What are you guys doing here?' he asked.

"Oh Colt honey, we were so worried about you. Are you okay?" asked Leona.

"Why worry? I was just going to go to class. I think I'm late or something," said Colt.

Robert took Colt by the arm and guided him toward the house. He looked at the others as if to say 'he isn't right'.

"Colt, let's go inside. We can talk better in there," said Robert with a tenderness he had never before exhibited.

"Uh okay. Er, uh, where is this? Where…" Colt started to say before stopping and staring into space.

"My baby, my baby. What's happened to my baby?" cried Leona.

Colt's body became limp, similar to a rag doll, forcing his father to exert more effort to support him. Robert guided him to his room as feelings of helplessness came over the group. Nobody wanted to comment on Colt's condition for fear of pointing out the obvious. Nobody wanted to admit that Colt was in real trouble.

It was late afternoon when they put Colt to bed. None of them had any idea what was wrong or how to proceed. Robert had seen similar symptoms in football games when a player was hit hard in the head. But, he had never heard of the symptoms lasting this long. He gathered the family and Bobby in the living room.

"Thanks Bobby for bringing him home. I am sure you need to get back to school. We can handle it from here," said Robert in a pleasant but authoritative manner.

The tone of Robert's words left no room for discussion. It was time for Bobby to leave. *Oh, if these guys only knew how little school has meant to me*, thought Bobby.

"Okay, I'll see you guys later then. I'll give it a while and then call," said Bobby.

Leona and Kelly thanked him with hugs. When he was gone, Robert spoke.

"Okay, here's the plan. I don't know what's wrong with him but we're going to keep Colt here overnight. If he isn't better in the morning, we'll go to the hospital. If something happens and he really looks bad we'll go sooner."

After no change in Colt's condition, they admitted him to Highline Hospital in Burien the next day. After a day of being looked at by various doctors and being given a few medications, his condition seemed the same if not worse.

In the room in Highline Hospital four worried faces looked down on Colt. His body was lying motionless on the bed, with eyes closed. He seemed peaceful as if he was in the middle of a hurricane with the emotions of the watchers swirling outside.

Colt's father mother and sister Kelly stared at him in desperation. Amy was crying quietly in a chair by the wall with her hands on her forehead. The doctor, a thin scrawny man with dark hair peppered with gray specks, had only minutes before walked out of the door. He left the group in a state of fear and loathing.

"What did he mean when he said he wasn't sure what might happen to Colt's brain? Crap, isn't this guy supposed to know this stuff?" asked Robert to nobody in particular.

Leona put her hands on Colt's head as tears formed in her eyes. The only person in the room who exuded any sense of being focused and functional was Kelly.

"Listen you guys. He said they didn't know much and that Colt might come out of it at any time. He hasn't been here that long. We need to think positive thoughts. I know I do, anyway," said Kelly.

"Oh honey, he seems so far away. And, he may never come back," said Leona as she broke into convulsive sobbing.

Robert put his arm around Leona and kissed her forehead. He looked at Kelly and spoke.

"Of course you're right sweetheart. It's just a shock. I thought they would figure this out and have a plan of action. It will take a while for us to get our bearings," said Robert.

Kelly hugged both of her parents and allowed a few tears to form in her eyes. *There is no way I am giving up. Whatever we have to do, we will,* she thought. After a few minutes she went over to Amy and sat by her. Amy had stopped crying but still seemed lost.

"Amy, let's get out of here and talk. Maybe we can figure out something. And, sitting here is driving me nuts," said Kelly.

"Uh, okay. Maybe we can call some people too. I need to find out just what happened," Any replied.

Leona was at home to check on things, shower and change clothes before returning to the hospital. After agonizing over Colt's condition, Leona remembered that Colt had mentioned Mrs. Carbon as someone who knew about Colt's special abilities.

Although she doubted that Mrs. Carbon could help Colt, she was at her wits end and was willing to try just about anything to help her son.

After answering the phone, Elyce settled in to talk to Leona. Both were mothers of teenage boys and found a basis for mutual understanding very quickly. When Leona started to talk about Colt's condition Elyce asked her a question.

"How did this happen to Colt?"

While she waited, Elyce slipped into a shallow psychic trance to pick up on hidden clues to Colt's condition.

"His friend Bobby said that he fell on a table and hit his back," answered Elyce.

"And you say he seems to be okay but not conscious?"

"Oh, I don't know about okay. But, his vital signs are not worse than when he went into the hospital."

Elyce sensed things about Colt but was not able to receive a clear picture of what was wrong.

"Do you mind if I visit? I'll need to place my hands on him. Is that okay?" asked Elyce.

"Are you a healer or something? Can you cure him?" asked Elyce hoping she would give her reason to be optimistic.

"I just want to see what's going on inside his head. I can't promise anything but if I can find out anything I'll let you know."

"Okay. Please stop by. Anything will be better than just waiting."

As soon as Leona hung up, Elyce called her friend Sasha.

"Get over here. We need to go to the hospital."

Elyce's friend Sasha stepped into the Carbon house. Unlike the petite red-haired Elyce, Sasha was rather tall with short black hair. When Elyce needed to use her psychic abilities, she always wanted her friend at her side. Sasha knew that Elyce would be in some psychic zone and not able to drive. She also knew that when they arrived she would be the one who would pull Elyce back from her state of heightened awareness. It had always been this way, with one firmly grounded to the earth and one with a foot in another realm. Although Elyce could usually function perfectly well, when she opened up in this way, it was easy for her to become disconnected from normal consciousness.

After they pulled into the parking lot of Highline Hospital, Sasha lightly touched her friend's arm. She opened her eyes as she exhaled with a sigh. Tears formed in her eyes.

"That young man is not in a good place. He doesn't know how to get home. I may be able to help him but I need to see him first," said Elyce.

"Do we need to find a healer? Maybe someone who knows about auras?" asked Sasha.

"No. That won't help. He isn't connected to his body. I need to help him to get back into his body. Right now he is far away," she said.

They walked into the lobby of the hospital and Elyce was drawn to Amy and Kelly who were sitting on a large couch looking dejected. She looked at them and spoke.

"Are you with Colt O'Brien? I'm Mr. Carbon's wife Elyce and this is my friend Sasha," said Elyce.

"Yes, I'm Kelly his sister and this is Amy, his girlfriend. How did you know?" asked Kelly.

"I just had a feeling," said Elyce as she hugged both of the young women.

Chapter 28

------**Email**-------
From: Sims, Tasha[TSims@wwu.edu]
To: Alioto, Megan[MAlioto@wwwu.edu]
Subject: Bobby Jones

Wow
After Bobby's friend got hurt, I haven't seen him. After partying all year, it's like empty without him around. He sure became a wild child after being so straight and narrow. He'll come back. They all do.

T

------**Email**-------

Bobby Jones sat across from a pleasant looking man with a crew cut and soft olive colored eyes. They were in a small office on campus. Bobby's hands were shaking slightly and his entire body had a damp sweaty feeling. He felt dirty even though he had just taken a shower. After living through the crisis with Colt and blaming himself, Bobby had vowed that he would seek help. After not having a drink for almost two days, doubts about his decision were creeping in. Now, he only wanted a big gulp of something with alcohol. Wine, beer, whiskey, it didn't really matter that much.

After sitting across from Don Parkington, for a few minutes, Bobby was becoming irritated. *Isn't this guy going to say anything? I'm going nuts here.* Just when he was about to the bolt from the room, Don smiled and spoke.

"Hi Bobby. You didn't tell me what you wanted to talk about when you made the appointment. But, after seeing you I'm pretty sure I can figure that out all on my own," said Don with a firm stare.

"I look that bad, huh?"

"I'm going to simplify this for you. I had an alcohol problem. I got it fixed and I know all about your situation and the one way to deal with it. "

"Uh, yeah, I screwed up but there must be an easy way to deal with a little boozing?" asked Bobby who was surprised by the sudden confidence of his counselor.

"You're an alcoholic. There's no easy way, no shortcut and no fun in getting sober. I know you have a lot of reasons and excuses but take my advice and forget all of that crap. Save your energy for the battle ahead."

Bobby thought about the strong words and the direct approach of the counselor. *No way I'm an alkie. This guy is just wrong about me*, thought the shaky student.

"Listen, I just got into this partying thing when I got to college. It's not my fault. I know there's an easy way to handle this," said Bobby.

Don smiled a knowing smile. Bobby felt his sincerity but was still confused.

"It's a little bit like getting sick. Once you do, steps need to be taken to get better. Some people can take or leave alcohol. A certain percentage of people can't handle it at all. For them, it's like having the flu all the time," said Don.

"What do you mean? I'm not sick. It's just a rough patch," said Bobby.

"Your problem is drinking. Everything in your file and everything I've heard points to that. You're going through withdrawals now because you stopped. If you don't get help for the problem, you'll be back drinking soon."

Bobby breathed in and pushed his chest out to express strength. The counselor recognized that it was false bravado and smiled a knowing smile.

"I can quit the drinking and partying anytime. No problem. No problem at all. I think we've talked enough," yelled Bobby.

Don looked at the sickly young man with compassionate eyes. He remembered sitting in the same chair that Bobby was in and saying similar things.

"Here's the deal. There is help for you when you are ready to admit you have a problem. It's up to you. If you can quit the booze so easily then do it and see me in a week or so. Then, we can look at other things. But, until you get the drinking handled, you're wasting my time and yours.

"You're full of crap. I don't know why you are saying these things but I'm not buying it," yelled Bobby as he turned toward the door.

"I'm here if you change your mind," said Don Parkington.

~~~

Bobby was back in his dorm room. *No way that Don guy knows crap. How can he?* He saw the man as another stupid bureaucrat who had a rule book to follow. When he sat down in a chair to try to absorb what he was told and how to proceed, he remembered that Colt was in the hospital and he was alone. He could not stop the feelings of guilt and loneliness from rising up.

He knew he should eat something and get some rest but he became physically ill when he even thought about food. After an hour in the room, as darkness crept in, he'd had enough. *I'll go find some people and have a little fun. That will cheer me up*, he thought.

The night was fun and alcohol-free for awhile. Eventually Bobby ran into Tasha and Megan, his favorite party pals. In spite of his desire to avoid booze, the girls were very persuasive and seemed to be on his side. They were sympathetic to his feelings of guilt and made him feel at peace with himself.

Tasha grabbed his arm, pulled him close and gave him a kiss on the lips.

"I missed you. It makes me sad to see you like this. Let us cheer you up. Let's cruise around and find some fun," said Tasha.

"Yeah but I need to take it easy on the booze," said Bobby.

"Hey, nobody's going to force you to drink. You make your own decisions," said Megan with a smile.

"Let's go then," said Bobby.

It took exactly 1 hour and 16 minutes before Bobby's first drink. He didn't stop enjoying himself until the early morning as the sun was about to rise. When he woke in the afternoon of the next day, Tasha was sleeping next to him. His head was pounding and he felt overcome with nausea. After being sick for the remainder of the afternoon, Bobby called Don Parkington. The kind man answered the phone.

"I'm glad you called Bobby. Let's get to work."

Chapter 29

------Email-------
From: O'Brien, Leona[LeonaB@aol.com]
To: Wise, Deborah[DebbieW@aol.com]
Subject: So worried

Hi Deb

I am sooo worried about Colt. The doctors don't seem to have a clue. And my husband looks scared too. That never happens.
Pray for my baby.

Leona

------Email-------

Elyce Carbon stood next to Colt's hospital bed with her hand resting lightly on his forehead. Her friend Sasha with Kelly and Amy stood as far away as the small room would allow. Sasha held her finger with a bright pink fingernail over her lips to indicate that they should all be quiet. Amy looked on with fear while Kelly seemed curious.

After closing her eyes, Elyce, with her diminutive stature and bright red hair, lifted her arms with the flat palms of her hands pointing to the side of Colt. She slowly moved along his body as if she was feeling around in the dark. She stopped a few times on her way to Colt's feet. Although she did not touch Colt's body, the three women felt that there was an invisible connection between her and the comatose young man in the bed.

After about ten minutes, Elyce opened her eyes and sat on a chair next to the bed. She seemed far away. Sasha walked over and placed her hand on Elyce's shoulder. That seemed to bring her to a more wakeful state. Still, it took her a few minutes to refocus herself to the point where she could communicate with the others.

"Sorry about that. I traveled a long way to find him. It takes me a while to come back again," said Elyce.

Both Amy and Kelly were wondering what she meant by travel when Sasha spoke.

"I can see this is new to you two. All you need to know is that she sees things that we can't see. And, she may be the only hope for Colt to come back to us."

Kelly didn't really know what was happening but she was ready to hear anything that would bring her brother back.

"Uh, what did you see," asked Kelly to encourage Elyce to share her findings.

"I will try to explain it to you but I have to keep it simple," said Elyce.

The girls perked up when they thought that she could tell them something.

"Colt is in, what we call the astral plane. It's like different psychic levels with the higher being more spiritual and the lower being more earthly. Somehow he became trapped in one of the lowest places," said Elyce.

"Is that bad?" asked Amy.

"It's like if you went to Normandy Park to visit someone and you ended up in a third world country. He's surrounded by fear, hate and dark, earthly desires."

"What can we do?" asked Kelly.

"I see that his lower chakra was opened up. Whatever happened to him was like a nuclear explosion. I'll have to meditate at home and see if I can do something. If I can't figure something out, I'll ask for help. I suggest you put an ice pack on the base of his spine. You'll see that it's still very hot. It may help."

"Uh, when will you know something? Can't the doctors do anything?" asked Amy.

"I doubt it. Sasha has your numbers. I'll call, no matter what, in a day or two. Now I have to go," answered Elyce.

"Thanks" said Kelly.

Sasha and Elyce left. When they were in the car on the way home, Sasha turned to her friend.

"How bad is it?"

"It's bad. It's really bad."

~~~

Elyce and Sasha sat in the front room of the Carbon home. Whenever Elyce looked up at the clouds painted on the ceiling, she became light-headed. She was still feeling the effects of her visit to the astral plane to find Colt.

"Please stay for awhile. I need you here to help me stay grounded. Once I get my energy back, I'll see if I can locate that poor boy again," said Elyce.

Sasha smiled. She was happy that her friend needed her and that she was a part of something good. Both of the women had their own talents. They complemented each other.

"I'll stay as long as you need me. I think when you try to find Colt again, I should be here. I know it takes a lot out of you when you leave your body like that," said Sasha.

Elyce remembered the one time that she went too far and couldn't find her way back into her body. Sasha was able to bring her back.

"Listen, I think I'm okay now but I've done enough for today. Nobody will be here tomorrow. Could you come back then?" asked Elyce.

"Sure, but you take it easy. I can tell you are still not totally grounded. I'll come over tomorrow morning."

Elyce hugged Sasha who then left.

The next morning Elyce sat in her overstuffed chair in the front room of her light purple house. She was surrounded by antique furniture and old pictures that helped her to find the serenity she needed to feel safe and calm. Sasha sat close at her side.

"I was able to rest last night. I'm ready. But if you feel like I'm in trouble, pull me back," said Elyce.

"I'll be watching," said Sasha,

Elyce closed her eyes and slipped into a meditative state. Soon she eased out of her earthly body. Sasha, who sat at her side, inhaled deeply when her friend left the earthly plane and entered into the other side.

After about a half hour Sasha sensed that her friend was near. Elyce, with eyes still closed, leaned toward Sasha and gently grabbed her arm. As usual, Sasha could feel the solid connection that aided Elyce in her return to this world. After a few minutes, Elyce opened her eyes, which were glowing with spiritual light.

"We need to go to the hospital," was all that she said.

Chapter 30

------Email-------
From: O'Brien, Robert[ROBrian@aol.com]
To: Norman, Ted[TNorman@yahoo.com]
Subject: My son

Hello Ted

My son Colt is still in a deep coma. The doctors seem to be worthless. I've never felt so helpless to do anything in my life.

Bob

------Email-------

Leona O'Brien watched as Elyce Carbon leaned over Colt who still lay peacefully in the hospital bed. Her friend Sasha stood shoulder to shoulder with her. Elyce held a small dark bottle in her delicate hand. In a momentary break in the stream of visitors, nurses, and doctors, it was just the three of them. Leona's fears and depression had not stopped since Colt went into the coma, but now for some reason, a calm internal cloud soothed her. *Oh, what nice red hair that lady has*, she thought. Elyce's bright red hair seemed to emit a healing current that permeated the small sterile room. For the first time, Colt's mother was hopeful and was not thinking about the worst that might happen.

Elyce leaned closer to Colt who had a serene look on his face. As she did Sasha moved with her making sure that their shoulders remained in contact. Elyce put one hand on Colt's

149

forehead. She placed the small open bottle under his nose. Then, she whispered in his ear. One of Colt's hands twitched. Leona jumped up with her hands clenched and watched hoping that her world would be made whole again. Elyce and Sasha swayed in unison, ever so gently, as Elyce continued to whisper in Colt's ear. Now a faint smell of eucalyptus was evident to everyone in the room. After a time Elyce set down the bottle and removed her hand from Colt's forehead. She placed both of her hands over his head with the palms facing down. Slowly, she moved them down his body toward his feet without touching him.

In a flash Colt inhaled deeply and bolted upright with his eyes wide open. He seemed disoriented and not aware of his surroundings. He scanned the room but still seem out of it. Elyce hugged him and gently pushed him back down. She backed away then turned to Leona and gently spoke.

"Give him a few minutes to adjust. He came to us from far away."

Leona sat back down and sobbed. Sasha held on to her friend who was having a difficult time staying upright. As Sasha and Elyce turned toward the door, Colt spoke.

"Thank you. I was so lost. You showed me how to get back."

Elyce turned around. She smiled as tears began to form in her sea-blue eyes.

"You rest and get used to being back. We can talk later after I recover and recharge my old batteries."

The two women walked out the door as Kelly and Amy walked in. When they saw that Colt was awake, they rushed to his side.

"Give him some time girls," said Leona through a waterfall of tears. "My baby's back."

~~~

After being released from the hospital and resting at home for a few days, Colt sat in the living room of his Normandy Park home. His sister Kelly had returned to school as had Amy. Leona and Robert O'Brien sat facing him intent on hearing the rest of the story about his experience. Colt had already told them about how he ended up in a coma and was now moving on to explain what his out-of-body experience was like.

"So, I don't remember it as one long thing. It's like a movie of highlights with lots of blank spots," said Colt.

"Oh honey it must have been terrible. We don't need to talk about it if you don't want to," said Leona.

"It's okay. A lot of it was like a really bright dream. Anyway, I was moving toward a bright light when I felt like I was pulled to the side. Then it was like I was surrounded by bad things. I couldn't help being afraid."

"Why were you afraid, Colt," asked his father.

"I don't know. It was like I was surrounded by waves of fear that I was absorbing. And, I had no sense of time or where I was. I felt sad, lost and forgotten," said Colt.

Leona cringed as she envisioned Colt disconnected from her love. The feelings she felt when Colt was in that hospital bed came flooding back to her. She realized that she felt him even though his body showed no signs of awareness.

"How did you get away from all of that?" asked Robert.

"I don't know how long it was but eventually something got my attention. It was like a little firefly flitting around. It was bright and had a sort of purplish color. Once I concentrated on it, I started moving. It was like slowly moving out of a muddy swamp. Oh I know. It was like being pulled out of quicksand."

"What happened next?" asked Leona.

"Suddenly the firefly thing was in front of what seemed to be a huge sun. But the light wasn't like the real sun. Then the firefly was gone. I felt the sun strengthening me. And, then I woke up."

Robert smiled with a mix of understanding and relief which surprised Colt.

"I've seen guys in football games get knocked out and tell similar stories when they came around. I'm just glad you came out of it still able to think straight. Usually they have concussions," he said.

"Yeah Dad, but they got hit on the head. I was hit on my spine. I don't think it was a concussion." said Colt.

"I'm just glad you're okay." said his father who truly was relieved.

"That's enough talk about it. We love you Colt and that's all you need to know," said Leona as she rushed to hug him.

"Yeah, I think I'm ready to give it a rest. But, I'm happy I got it all out," said Colt.

Colt remembered his talk with Elyce Carbon about his experience. When she explained it, it all made sense. He knew that she was the little firefly and that she helped him to find his way back. To Colt, she saved his life. He also knew that he needed to follow her advice and learn more about his psychic abilities and how to use them correctly.

Chapter 31

------Email-------
From: Webmaster [Webmaster@guruboy.com]
To: O'Brien, Colt[ColtOB@yahoo.com]
Subject: Let's talk

COLT

I LOOK FORWARD TO HEARING ABOUT YOUR EXPERIENCES.
I WILL CALL YOU IN THE AFTERNOON AS WE DISCUSSED.

GURUBOY

------Email-------

Colt had only been back at school for a few days after his hospital stay. Before he moved back into going at full speed he had one thing to take care of. It was Sunday afternoon, the only time when Colt seemed to be able to relax and unwind. In the morning he had been with Amy but now he was doing as little as possible in hopes that he could store up enough energy for the week ahead. The call he was expecting had not come, which made him curious but not agitated. So many things irritated him, on a daily basis, that he was learning to take everything in stride. Although this was not work or school related, it was another item on his internal list of things to do. *If the dude calls, he calls*, thought Colt with little concern. However, he did wonder what clues this internet spiritualist would give him about his special abilities and, most of all, how to avoid getting into trouble. *I wonder if he can explain all this weird stuff that happens to me?*

Colt thought of making some coffee but laid his head on a cushion on the couch instead. In seconds he was in a deep sleep.

Colt soon was dreaming. Scenes came and went in a disjointed fashion. When a large red serpent slipped into his dreamscape, Colt remembered something from his past but couldn't make it clear in his mind. One thing was certain. This vision resulted in extreme fear causing him to wake up with a start. The phone was ringing making his entrance into a wakeful state even more jarring. After a few seconds, while he oriented himself, Colt answered.

"Uh yeah."

"Hello, is this Colt O'Brien?" asked a quiet voice.

"Yeah, sorry I just woke up. Can you call back in a few minutes? I'm like spaced out."

Colt made some strong coffee and waited for the call. He knew that the vision of his dream had some deeper meaning. *Maybe this guy can tell me about the red snake. I don't even know his real name.* Colt found that guruboy's name was Alexander Sarkin. First, Colt provided some background to his caller with some references to his special abilities. Then, it was Colt's turn to ask questions.

"So, you must really know a lot? Where did you learn about this stuff?" asked Colt.

"So, I've done a lot of traveling, reading and mostly searching. It helps me to digest it all by having the web site," said Alexander.

"For me it's totally different. All this stuff just seems to happen. I don't know how. I don't do yoga or any of that stuff," said Colt.

"I think you were just born with certain abilities. How about if we try a few eastern yoga techniques just to see what happens?" asked Alexander.

"Okay. What about your phone bill?"

"Don't worry about that. I have it covered."

After Alexander had Colt sit in various yoga poses and do special breathing techniques, Colt could feel his chakra centers humming with vibrancy.

"Okay, now I want you to try to stimulate the kundalini chakra at the base of the spine. Just close your eyes and think of a spinning ball of energy. It should begin to expand in power."

"What is kundalini? It sounds dark to me," asked Colt.

"It's a potential force that can give you insight into spiritual things. It's the chakra at the base of the spine. We're trying to awaken it."

"Uh okay. I'm thinking about a ball of energy. It's growing really fast," said Colt.

"Now, see that ball slowly moving up the spine."

Before Colt could do as directed, a flash of bright light hit him as if from a sun within his head. At the same time the ball of energy at the base of his spine overwhelmed him casing nausea and confusion. He fell onto his back on the floor, immobilized. As he fought to gain his equilibrium, he saw the huge red serpent from his previous dream. He felt guided to a place of calmness and thought he heard an inner voice.

The voice only said 'Turn off the lights.'

Instinctively, Colt knew to make the base chakra less bright and less powerful by focusing on it in a certain way. As the power of kundalini lessened Colt was able to slowly regain his awareness of the world around him and sit up. Alexander was screaming on the cell phone which was on the floor. Colt picked it up.

"Uh, what did you do to me? And why did I see the snake?" he asked.

"What happened? You saw a snake?" asked a concerned Alexander.

"Uh yeah. I saw a flashing light and that energy thing just exploded. Then I saw the big red snake. It was smothering me," answered Colt.

"I have some checking to do. This is great. You have a gift. I think that you just pushed it a bit too much. You'll get better at this.

Colt was beginning to feel like himself again and was not into any more experimenting.

"Dude, I had no control. And, I started to feel like that snake is out to get me. I have to go. Later," said Colt as he hung up.

After Colt hung up, the effects of his psychic experience lingered. At times he felt like his feet were floating above the floor of his dorm room. Also, he would have flashbacks of the huge red snake and his recent out of body experience. He started to shake with fear. *Maybe some strong coffee will help. I've had enough of this weird crap for one day.*

As he made the coffee, Colt wondered if he would ever get control of the special powers that he had. Because of his past experience, he knew that practice was necessary to become proficient at anything. Also, having the proper coaching was crucial. *I wonder if that voice I heard was real or just in my head. It reminded me of a soccer coach I had once.*

Drinking his coffee and pondering his recent experience, had a calming effect on Colt. He sensed that he needed the proper guidance from someone with experience in the area of psychic experience. *But, how am I going to find someone who is good at this stuff.* Just when he was about to mentally move on to less taxing thoughts, a face formed in his mind. Delicate rays of light emanated from the face causing him to feel that everything would be okay. After a short time he was able to see past the light. The face of Elyce Carbon emerged penetrating his mind and soul.

Chapter 32

------Email-------
From: Girl, Psuedo[psuedogirl@aonymous.net]
To: Anonymous, Mr.[mranon@anonymous.net]
Subject: hacker guy

```
Hi
We have a mutual friend in John Freeman.  I have
followed your cool doings on the web for awhile.
Wondering if we could meet to talk about common
interests.  John didn't tell me much about you except
that you liked your privacy.  So this meeting thing is
all up to you.
I am a programmer based in Redmond, and do a lot of
international network stuff.  I would love to pick your
brain.  I can tell you more about me if you want to
know.  I'm sorta known on the net too.
Let me know what you think.
PsuedoGirl

Yes, I really am a girl.  Well......a grown up girl.
```

------Email-------

Fletcher Rowe sat in a chair in his tiny dorm room in the early evening. He was surrounded by computer equipment that hummed and emitted an occasional high pitched beep. On his lap was a laptop computer with a large screen flipped up for viewing. A long cable ran from the side of the small machine to the back of one of the other larger computers. Fletcher stared at the screen with red, tired eyes above a two-day old growth of light whiskers. His stringy blond hair cried out for a thorough washing. He was used to going days where he slept little, but now it was time to recharge. *One last check of email and then I'll crash. Man, am I burned out. Hmm, this looks interesting.* Fletcher read the email from someone with an online name of pseudogirl. His experience with the opposite sex was limited and he viewed any personal interaction with girls as a scary, treacherous journey to a foreign land. The desire was there, but unlike with computers, he felt inept and blind with girls. Until recently, he had found it easier to just avoid dealing with girls. But now, he felt desire bubbling up on a regular basis. When he did leave his computer-filled dorm room, which was not often, he found himself entranced with young co-eds that he encountered. Without thinking much about it, he wrote an email to pseudogirl.

Hi Pseudogirl

I've heard of you too. Let's talk on the phone and set something up. Please send me your number.

F

Fletcher clicked on the Send button in his email program and the email was gone. He was calm for a minute and then a queasy ball of doubt formed in his gut. Fear rushed up causing him to visualize worst case scenarios. After not eating much and living on coffee, his state of mind was susceptible to flights of fancy. The possible outcomes that he conjured up were extreme and disastrous. He knew that he was not really very awake when he sent the email. Although it was a reaction that came out of loneliness, lack of sleep and sexual desire, he just saw himself as an idiot. After thinking about it for a few minutes he tried to get a grip on his emotions. *Shit! Here I am burned out and I send an email to a girl who I don't even know. At least I hope it's a girl. I never should have done it without more thought and research. I better go to sleep before I do some other stupid thing.*

Fletcher woke up at around noon of the next day after sleeping as if in a coma. It had been fifteen hours of mostly dreamless sleep. He stretched his thin frame and listened to the rain splattering against his dorm room window. After making coffee and eating a bowl of cereal, he felt an itch in the back of his mind. *Something happened before I crashed. Hmmm. Oh shit, pseudogirl.*

Wearing only boxer shorts and a t-shirt Fletcher logged on and opened his email. He found what he sought immediately. The email was short.

```
Hi F whatever that means
    I don't want my number going out in email.  You
know how it is.  Let's just do a chat.  OK?  Just
find pseudogirl on instant messenger.
    P
```

Fletcher smiled while reading the note. *I guess she's smart enough to ignore my stupid note and do things the right way. But now I have to deal with a babe. This should be fun. Aaaahhhh!*

After taking a shower, shaving, and brushing his teeth, Fletcher felt like a new man. A good night's sleep made him feel like he could function at optimum capacity for a long period of time. His paranoid delusions were under control and he felt like he was ready to face anything. *If I can chat with a cyber-babe, I can do anything.* After a long walk around campus, he returned with a large paper cup of black coffee and a bag of donuts.

He grabbed a laptop PC and booted it up. He opened a network utility application and started to check network activity which he did at least once daily. His eyes widened as text scrolled from the bottom of the screen to the top. He tapped a key stopping the data from moving and pored over the stationary text on the screen. At the same time the other computers began to beep in short intervals. *Shit, I was afraid of that. This is not good. And I was feeling so great, too.* He quickly jumped up and flipped a switch on the power strip on the floor causing all of his machines to unceremoniously shut down leaving a faint humming sound throughout the room. He proceeded to unhook wires from the computers that were attached to a small rectangular box on the floor.

At least now I'm not hooked up to the network. Maybe I can protect my computers and then do some research.

After installing a firewall program on one of the tower computers, he opened the options list for the program. He made some modifications. Then he shut down the computer and plugged it back into the network. After he was up and running again on only one computer, he typed in a few words and watched. After about ten minutes, he looked to the ceiling in frustration and spoke.

"This could get ugly. And, all of my testing could get trashed."

Chapter 33

------Email-------
From: O'Brien, Colt[ColtOB@yahoo.com]
To: Carbon, Billy[billg@hocs.biz]
Subject: hacker guy
----

hey dude
A while back I worked a ticket and ended up in this guys dorm room. he
had two laptops and two desktops hooked together.it was overloading
the network. after I got there he hit a few keys and the problem
disappeared. I never did figure out what he was up to. any ideas?
Colt

------Email-------

The two weeks that Colt missed were a like a giant black hole into which school and work tasks were haphazardly dumped. The days he was gone now seemed like years as he tried to catch up with his studies and computer work. Although he was behind on school assignments, Amy had been getting the assignments he needed and helping him where she could. However, it looked like trouble tickets for Windows PCs had sat idle, as if frozen in time, while he was away.

On top of everything else, his out of body experience was not that easy to assimilate. It felt like a huge river of experience had flowed into him but his brain did not have enough capacity to process everything. When he tried to categorize experiences, he became confused and frustrated. It was only when he let go and did not try to categorize things, that gems of understanding were revealed. In spite of the severity of his near-death, out-of-body experience, Colt felt optimistic most of the time.

Somehow he knew that life would be fine if he only relaxed and let it come to him. However, he noticed that those who loved him were still concerned. He discovered soon after his ordeal that acting too nonchalant caused some people to worry.

When he had finally readjusted to school, with his new outlook on life, and was almost caught up with schoolwork, he was ready to tackle the job of fixing computers. After his history with Gerry, Colt almost expected that he would be fired after being gone for so long. Gerry surprised him by acting like everything was business as usual. Colt still thought that he was hoping for a reason to get rid of him for good. *I guess he still he needs me. Probably none of his UNIX guys want to do the work I do. With all these tickets I might burn out anyway. I need to get them to give me some help.*

It was the end of the school day and Colt was ready to relax. Bobby was still in rehab, so he had the room to himself. Just as he was thinking about what would relax him the most, his pager began beeping mercilessly. *Goddamn it. Not now. I really, really am not into this right now.* He looked at the text on the tiny pager screen. 'Call me, Gerry' was all that was displayed. *Hey, maybe he's only going to give me another one of his stupid lectures. This could be okay,* thought Colt. But beneath his optimism, deep in his gut, he suspected something alarming was about to hit him. When Gerry answered the phone, Colt knew for sure that this was not going to be fun.

"Yeah, this is Gerry," he said as if he was mad at the world.

"Uh, hi, this is Colt. You needed something?"

"You're damn right I need something. Half of the Windows PCs started having problems about an hour ago. And, you're the only guy I've got."

"Well, usually when it's that many computers hosed up, it's a network problem. I'll check it out," said Colt hoping he was right.

"If it's the network then you're the luckiest tech guy in the world. Just fix it," snarled Gerry.

"Okay, Gerry. I'm on it," said Colt.

Colt guessed that there were numerous tickets and decided to go to the tech room and talk to the dispatchers. *Maybe I can get a better feel for what types of problems are happening.* He grabbed his equipment bag with his laptop and tools. He was soon trotting in rain toward the tech room. As he neared the building he was heading for, his cell phone rang. Colt hurried along until he was inside and answered.

"Uh, you may not remember me but this is Fletcher Rowe."

"Oh, yeah, I remember. You had all the hardware in your room," answered Colt.

"Well, it's all disconnected from the network now because of the problems."

"Yeah, I'm going to work on those problems right now. So, I'm sorta busy. You didn't do something weird did you?" asked Colt who was now a bit suspicious.

"Uh no. It wasn't because of me. But, if you want some help fixing it, I have been checking around and found out some stuff."

Colt remembered the last time he was with Fletcher. He knew that the hacker had caused the network problem that affected an entire building.

"Listen, I haven't even seen the tickets yet. I have to see what's happening before I start doing stuff for you. I'll call you if I need help."

"Uh okay, but…" he started to say.

But Colt had hung up.

Man, I hope this guy wises up. He'll need all the help he can get, thought Fletcher.

When Colt arrived at the tech room, the two young female dispatchers were answering phones. Both of them seemed frantic. When Colt walked over, the one named Janice put a caller on hold and turned to him.

"Goddamn users. They can be so rude. Screw them all," she yelled as she slammed the phone down.

"Uh, hi Janice. What's going on? What types of problems are you seeing?" asked Colt.

"You name it. Files missing, email, PCs rebooting. The only common thing is that it's all Windows PCs," she said.

"Uh, how many tickets do you have?"

"We stopped taking tickets after about a hundred. We figured that sending them all to your pager would be a waste."

"I guess you better send me ten or 15 tickets. I'll start looking at computers and see what I can find out."

After receiving the first ticket, Colt set his pager to vibrate and left. As he walked to the location of the problem, he allowed himself to slip into a meditative start. As his chakras lit up and pulsed, he had a vision. Millions of tiny spiders were being carried through wires and phone lines to any PC attached to the network. Then the spiders scurried through every system on the machine poisoning them. Colt called Fletcher Rowe.

The first words out of the hacker's mouth were, "It's the Black Widow virus."

Chapter 34

------Email-------
From: O'Brien, Colt[ColtOB@yahoo.com]
To: Jones, Bobby[Bobbyj@WWU.edu]
Subject: When are you getting out?

Hey Bobinator
I know it's tough going through rehab. Were all impressd and rooting for you. If you want a job to keep you busy when you get out, let me know. These guys just keep piling more crap on but no help. Hope to see you soon.
Dude, hang in there
Colt

------Email-------

Shit, the Black Widow virus is bad news. I could be really screwed this time. As soon as Colt hung up from Fletcher's call his mind raced to concoct a plan; so many questions popped up that he was stunned into inaction. Fletcher had only said that he was doing research and that this was a bad virus. Only when he calmed down enough to focus on the first steps, did he realize that he needed help. Colt didn't know a lot about the Black Widow virus but he did know that even big companies with large IT departments were brought to their knees when it attacked their Windows computers.

As he began walking again to the location of his first trouble ticket, he realized that his original course of action was a waste of time. *I need to know more before I do anything. I could just make it worse if I don't have a plan.* Colt quickly turned around and headed toward his dorm room which was nearby. As he walked he wondered who he could enlist to help him. *I don't trust that hacker guy. Man, I wonder what that dude is really into with all that computing power.* After sitting down and plugging in his laptop, he called the most tech-savvy person he knew.

"Hi. This is Billy."

"Hey little dude. This is Colt. I need some help," said Colt to Billy Carbon.

"Yeah, no problem. Let me guess. It's a Windows virus?" answered Billy.

"You got it. I have PCs with lots of problems all over the place."

"It seems like every day there's another crappy virus to fix. Well if it's the Black Widow virus, there's a fix on the Microsoft site. You can push it out to the PCs on your network, but you need to do a little programming. And, the computers that aren't on the network need to have someone log on to the machine to load the fix."

"Yeah, it's the Black Widow thing. At least there's a way to fix it. But, it sounds like a lot of work for just one guy. And, I don't know much programming," said Colt.

"We can't help you either. We have other stuff going on. Except on the phone a little," said Billy.

"I better download that fix and start working on this. You've been a big help. I might call you later."

"Yeah, you'll be busy. It's no fun at all."

"Later," said Colt.

"Later," said Billy.

Colt logged onto the Microsoft site and downloaded the virus software fix with instructions on how to use it, which seemed easy enough. *No way I can put this on all of the PCs alone.* As he pondered his situation, he pictured Fletcher Rowe. It was as if a vivid movie was playing in his head. He saw the hacker writing lines of programming code at a very fast rate. Somehow Colt knew that this computer nerd, who lurked in the shadows, was the key to his success. *I guess I better call this guy, even though I don't know if I should trust him.* Colt had his cell phone in his hand, ready to call, when it rang.

"Hello."

"Hey Colt, this is Mr. Carbon. I just talked to Billy about your situation. I bet you're feeling a bit overwhelmed about now," said Matthew Carbon.

"Uh, hi. Yeah, it's a lot to deal with. And, this is the first time I've had this many machines infected," answered Colt.

"I know you are concentrating on fixing problems but there is something more important that you need to think about."

"Uh, er, what?" asked Colt.

Colt waited hoping that Mr. Carbon wasn't going to give him more work to do.

"You need to tell that UNIX boss of yours what is going on and what you are going to do. That way if bad things happen, he won't be able to say that you went behind his back. Any steps you take need to be communicated to him. I'm guessing that if things don't go well, he will try to blame everything on you.

"Wow, I was so into fixing things that I didn't even think about Gerry. And, I know you're right. He's just itching to find a way to get rid of me," said Colt.

"That's all I had for you. Tell him what it is and that you are too understaffed to fix it. If he doesn't give you any help, then it's on him when all the hard questions come up."

"Thanks Mr. Carbon. I may try to recruit some guys to help me. I'll tell him what has to happen and how long it could take with me doing it all. I'll let you know how it goes."

"Good deal. And, call Billy if you get stuck on the technical stuff."

~~~

When Colt called Gerry he was still belligerent until Colt explained the situation in detail. He reluctantly allowed Colt to recruit a few people for the project, after realizing that he might have to assign his UNIX workers to help work on Windows computers.

~~~

Fletcher Rowe sat in a beanbag chair looking up at Colt. He had an unopened laptop computer lying next to him. Colt noticed that he didn't like to make eye contact and had to force himself to talk directly to him. *This must be important to mysterious hacker guy for him to come out of his cave to work with me*, thought Colt.

"Uh, okay Fletch. I guess we need a program to push out the fix to the machines on the network. And, we need a team to go to the other PCs," said Colt.

"Please call me Fletcher. Well, it may not be that easy," replied the fragile hacker.

Colt felt like he was talking to a person made of glass. One wrong move and Fletcher Rowe might shatter. *I better help this guy mellow out or he will be useless*, thought Colt.

"Uh, er, sure, Fletcher. I know that maybe I made it sound simpler that it really is. But let's try to do the simple stuff first. Can you write the program we need?"

The nerd seemed to brighten at Colt's question. It seemed to Colt that his new helper was expecting to be put down in some way. *Man, I don't think this guy can read people very well.* When Colt treated him as an asset of a team rather than a social outcast, Fletcher realized that his skills were valued. This treatment caused him to want to prove that he could have a positive impact on the situation. Fletcher smiled a timid smile and opened his laptop. After typing rapidly on the small keyboard he spoke.

"I already have a program written. I just need to do a little testing and go from there," said Fletcher.

"Wow, that's great," said Colt as he looked over Fletcher's shoulder at the code displayed on the screen.

"So, do you want me to go for it? Just get me access to the network and I'll go to work."

"Definitely, dude. This is awesome," said Colt

After some more discussion Colt requested another account that would be used for eradicating the virus. The account was given the proper security permissions to be able to access any Windows PC from the network. Fletcher obtained the virus fix from Colt and began testing and improving the program he had written. It seemed to Colt that the blond nerd went into a deep trance leaving the outer world behind as he worked. Just when he thought of asking Fletcher about his progress, the door opened and Bobby Jones walked in. It was a pleasant surprise to Colt when he saw that his friend was clear-eyed and healthy-looking.

"Bobinator, you're back. This is great. How do you feel?" asked Colt.

"Man, it was tough in the beginning but it feels great to be clean. I had to go to rehab just to find out how bad off I was," answered Bobby with a warm smile.

Colt noticed that Fletcher did not even look up. He ignored him and turned his full attention to his friend.

"Hey we have a lot to talk about. Let's go get some java. I'm recruiting guys to help with this virus thing. You are just the guy I need to help me on this job."

~~~

After spending hours obtaining information about the configuration of PCs on the network and refining his program, Fletcher was about to push the virus fix out to about 80% of the computers. Since it was now late and many of the target computers were turned off, Colt decided to start in the morning. He and Bobby would see how fast it went on individual PCs while Fletcher ran his network program.

When the time came Colt and Bobby sat in Fletcher Rowe's dorm room. The hum of cooling fans from the multiple computers filled the room as they looked over the programmer's shoulder.

"Uh, so the program will find whatever boxes are on the network and push out the fix and run it. It will write into a log file telling us if the little program worked or not. Then it will reboot the machine," said Fletcher.

Colt wondered if Fletcher had slept at all the night before. There were empty Coke cans and some half-eaten pizza on a table. However, the thin hacker seemed energized rather than tired.

"Uh okay. Let's do this," said Colt.

"Here goes," said Fletcher.

Colt expected to see fireworks of some kind but was surprised that the screen displayed nothing unusual. After about five minutes, Fletcher displayed a text file with short lines of information. At the end of each line was the word GOOD with a smiley face.

"Looks like we're okay guys. This should take about two hours," said Fletcher with a big grin.

171

Although it took about two weeks, eventually all the PCs on campus were inoculated from the Black Widow virus. Ninety percent were done in an hour and a half with the remainder taking almost the entire two weeks. Colt O'Brien and Bobby Jones became known and popular on campus as they met numerous students and fixed their computers. Fletcher Rowe lost interest after his program did its job but was happy that he could resume his own work beneath the computing radar.

Colt sat across from his friend Bobby in their dorm room. Both were drinking coffee. A fragrant cloud of rich coffee aromas engulfed them.

"Dude, we did good. It's like we went from being invisible except when bad crap happened to being campus heroes. And, we're not even on the football team," said Colt.

"Yeah, man. It was good for me too. I feel like I'm moving on from the problems I've had. Some of my teachers even noticed what we were doing." said Bobby.

"I needed you and you came through. I'd say you're back, baby, you're back."

Chapter 35

------Email-------
From: O'Brien, Colt[ColtOB@yahoo.com]
To: O'Brien, Kelly[Kellyobrien@UW.edu]
Subject: Party

Hi Kel
Can you get up here for this party? I did good on the virus thing and Bobby is out of rehab. would be great to see you.
Colt

------Email-------

Colt was enjoying himself. A small group of about twenty had gathered in his dorm room to celebrate his victory against the Black Widow virus. The crowd was crammed into the small space and overflowed into the hall. It was a Friday night and the students had the weekend to look forward to which made the crowd even more upbeat. In honor of Bobby Jones, no alcohol was present. Amy and her friend Suzy were there as well as friends of Colt. Gary Cable a huge football friend of Bobby's stood at the door to keep out party crashers. As a result, none of Bobby's old partying friends were there. Colt was pleased that his sister Kelly was able to attend. Her tall athletic figure and bright blond hair caused her to stand out. And, with her outgoing personality, she got along with everyone. A variety of tasty treats were on serving trays and in bowls. Flavored popcorn, brownies, and pizza slices were just a few of the foods. Large containers of rich, aromatic coffee littered the small room as well as exotic juices and pop. Colt sat in the middle of the

173

throng, holding court with stories about overcoming extreme computer problems and dealing with especially difficult customers. This was the perfect opportunity to embellish his accomplishments by adding the necessary color to the events. Colt had invited Billy Carbon and Gunnar Sweden, the high school student nerds that he used as advisors. *As long as they don't tell anybody how much they help me*, he thought. They were gawking at everything as if in a dream. One of Amy's friends even kissed Billy on the cheek and told him he was cute, causing the high school sophomore to blush multiple shades of red. After tracking down Fletcher Rowe by sending him a 911 message, Colt was able to talk him into making an appearance. To Colt this was a huge accomplishment.

Many in attendance were surprised when seeing Bobby for the first time after his rehab stint. He was almost not recognizable. His complexion was rosy and he had gained weight. His new appearance was accented by his attire which was neat and attractive. Suzy turned to Amy and whispered in her ear. Her eyes sparkled under jet black hair.

"Wow! Bobby looks really good. And happy too," she said.

"It just shows how far down he had gone. I am so happy for him," Amy whispered back.

"Now that he isn't around those party girls maybe he wants to date a real woman," said Suzy.

Amy smiled as she pictured her best friend with Bobby Jones.

"You go girl. But, you might have to transfer over here if it works out," said Amy with a smile.

Suzy winked at her friend and slowly moved toward Bobby. Amy batted her eyelashes teasing her friend.

As the party was slowing down with students leaving, Colt's cell phone rang playing the ring tone of the Beatle's song "Help". *Crap, it's like 11 at night. What the hell is this?*

"Yeah, this is Colt. What's up?"

"This is Gerry. There have been complaints about you. My boss has called a meeting of the department heads on Monday and he wants you to answer some questions."

Colt could feel his boss smiling behind the anonymity of the phone. He felt like screaming at him for destroying the good mood he was in. Through gritted teeth he spoke.

"Uh, er, uh, okay. When do I need to be there?" asked Colt.

"I will send you an email with the information. This could be the last meeting you're ever in with me," sneered Gerry.

Although Colt was composed he thought, *that would be my lucky day, you SOB.*

After hanging up on Gerry, Colt called Billy Carbon over.

"Hey Billy, when you get home tomorrow, tell your dad I need to talk to him soon," said Colt

"Yeah, sure. What about?"

"Politics," Colt replied.

~~~

Colt sat in a large conference room at a small table surrounded by about 15 Western Washington University department heads and faculty. Bobby Jones was at his side. Gerry was almost finished with his presentation of the complaints submitted by end-users. During the short presentation, some eyebrows were lifted at various times making Bobby a little nervous. To Colt it seemed like more of the same. *I don't know what the big deal is. There are always complaints like this.* Gerry, who was standing, looked down on Colt. He tried to be menacing without tipping off the panel but Colt was immune to his theatrics. *Yeah Gerry. Do your thing but don't get too confident you big dumb ass.*

"In conclusion, I would like to say that we have never seen this many complaints in such a short time. I only hope that we can salvage our reputation with our end-users," stated Gerry in a serious tone as he concluded his scathing speech and sat down.

The IT department head, Robert Snow, thanked Gerry and turned his potent gaze toward Colt. Colt was not used to being on stage when he had to explain his actions but he felt calm as he looked over his notes.

"Uh, how long do I have to present data from the outage that resulted in the complaints?" Colt read from a bold, underlined note.

"How long do you need Mr. O'Brien?" asked Robert Snow.

"I think twenty minutes should be enough," answered Colt.

Gerry turned red and started to speak but was stopped by a raised hand form his boss.

"Proceed Mr. O'Brien."

Bobby Jones had slipped away and was standing by a wall at the side of the room. He pulled down a screen and walked back to a laptop computer that was connected to a projector. Colt pointed to the screen.

"Everyone, please look at the screen. Okay Bobby, let's go," said Colt.

Man, am I happy that Mr. Carbon called. These notes are perfect. Just as he was about to start Colt remembered the last thing that Mr. Carbon told him.

"That guy is trying to screw you but you have to avoid going at him directly. The facts as you present them should be enough to get him into hot water. Just follow the script, keep it short and stick to the facts."

The script or outline consisted of three topics: What Colt did daily to support Windows PCs, the virus event, and the recent complaints. Since this was his first presentation, he decided early on that he would read from the script most of the time rather than adlib.

"Thank you for allowing me to present some facts. I'll try to keep this short and to the point," said Colt.

His presentation started by listing statistics about the number of computers that he supported, ticket counts and time spent. With each slide, Gerry's mood darkened. After the first section was done Colt scanned his audience.

"Up until the virus event, I was the only technologist supporting the more than 7000 personal computers on campus. I have no way to compare my performance with prior workers because there is no data. I will say this. It feels like I'm working an awful lot. Are there any questions before I continue?" asked Colt.

Colt's inner radar sensed that the level of surprise in the room was extremely high. The IT department head looked around the room getting a feel for the reaction of the panel. Then he stared at Gerry who was fidgeting in his chair.

"Did you work every ticket for the PC's, Colt?" he asked.

"Yes, I did," answered Colt.

"Please continue."

Colt continued, explaining in a step by step manner, the virus event. He remembered to thank Gerry for allowing him to recruit some help.

"So, luckily we were able to remove the virus over the network on ninety percent of the computers. Still, we had to touch almost 700 PCs." concluded Colt.

There were no questions but Colt's audience seemed a bit uneasy. *I wonder what's up with these guys. The vibe is sorta weird.*

Robert Snow's demeanor toward Colt was becoming better and better as indicated by his smile and body language. He also looked him straight in the eyes. *Is that respect, I'm feeling*, thought Colt.

"I'm very interested in the next part of your presentation, Mr. O'Brien. So far I've been intrigued," he said.

Colt started by displaying complaint statistics as compared to tickets. He showed the before and after.

"Although we did not create a ticket for every machine that had the fix applied, each machine had to be rebooted. So, each one was worked on in some manner. Even if we cut the ticket count in half, the number of complaints was far less by percentage for the virus event than before.

"So let me understand what you are saying. The three of you did this fix on over 7000 computers in about two weeks? Is that correct?" asked the department head.

"Uh yes sir. Fletcher Rowe did the network-attached computers and Bobby and I did the rest," answered Colt.

"I want to take this time to thank you and your helpers for your outstanding work. You may go now. Gerry, please stick around.

"Thanks again for letting me talk about what I do," said Colt.

He looked at Bobby who had the projector and laptop under his arm in carrying bags. His friend winked and they both turned for the door. Colt could not resist turning for one last look at Gerry. What he saw was a frightened man with a look of hopelessness in his eyes.

Chapter 36

------**Email**-------
From: Rowe, Fletcher[FRow@topmail.org]
To: Bates, Malcolm[MBates@topmail.org]
Subject: Almost there

```
Malcolm
I almost have the testing done.  I have written over 10000
lines of scripting code.  Just a little bit more until the
finish.

Fletcher
```

------**Email**-------

    Fletcher Rowe had pulled another all-nighter. It was 6 am and the bank of computers still hummed along in unison in his small dorm room. A special device called a network router camouflaged the number of computers he had running as well as what he was doing with them. Since the virus incident Fletcher had been monitoring what Colt was doing on the network. And, he occasionally hacked into the help desk database to look over tickets that Colt and Bobby Jones had worked. Although he was a loner, he was proud of his contribution to the resolution of the virus attack. Even though he didn't talk directly to Colt, he still felt like he was a part of the team. He had only a few friends and they were primarily hackers who were anti-social and anti-establishment. In spite of their influence, Fletcher wanted to move toward the establishment and away from lurking in the dark recesses of the internet. To him Colt, along with his friend John Freeman, was a connection with that world.

If those guys knew what I was doing here, they'd never believe it, he thought. *Just a few more months and I'll have it made. No more school, no more money worries. It'll be awesome.*

Fletcher was about to go to sleep when he saw an email alert marked urgent. He opened the email which was generated by a program he had written. The program automatically sent him an email if an event happened that was critical. Of course, what was important was decided by Fletcher. The email indicated that Colt and Bobby's email account had been accessed by someone else. *It's good that the security on this network is so bad. I can look at whatever I want,* thought Fletcher. After setting up a series of software traps to catch the intruder, he went to sleep.

The fragile nerd woke up in the early afternoon. He rarely attended classes. He had a system that included testing out of classes and self-study that allowed him to work primarily on his computer related projects. After getting a high-caffeinated pop from the small refrigerator, he looked at the results of his traps. He smiled as he called Colt.

"Yeah, this is Colt."

"Uh, hi Colt. This is Fletcher."

"Hey dude. I wondered if I would ever hear from you again. Don't you ever get out of that computer center you have in your dorm room?"

"Not much. I called because I'm seeing weird activity on the network."

Colt thought about how deep Fletcher delved into computers and wondered what 'weird' meant to him. *Why is he calling me? I hope it's not another virus.*

"Uh, er, what's weird?" asked Colt.

"Well, I sorta took you and Bobby under my wing after we teamed up. So, I watch to see how you are doing. I'm seeing someone hacking your email. I think they might be ready to use your account to send out messages. It might be important. It's hard for me to tell."

"Do you know who it is?"

"Looks like it's a guy named Gerry somebody."

"Uh oh. This can't be good. Can Bobby and I stop by to talk about this?"

Fletcher cringed a little when he thought about having guests but figured that it was his own fault.

"Uh, yeah. How about if we do a pizza night? You guys come over and we can get delivery. Is tonight good?"

"Yeah sure. We'll be there at seven and we'll bring the pizza. Later dude." said Colt.

After a busy day of attending classes and fixing computers, Colt and Bobby showed up at Fletcher's dorm room with pizza and a six-pack of pop in hand. Although Colt told Bobby about what to expect, he was stunned by the amount of computers in the small space. But, most of all, the loud humming noise made him feel like he entered another world. And, Colt was right. To Bobby it felt like a small data center.

Fletcher looked the part of a nerdy hacker shut away from the world. He wore plaid pajama bottoms, with a black t-shirt and purple slippers. His long blond hair was a tangled mess. Colt and Bobby sat in two metal folding chairs in the middle of the room. Fletcher sat in a large fancy office chair on wheels. *I bet that guy lives in that chair*, thought Colt. Colt opened the conversation after realizing that Fletcher wasn't going to say anything unless prodded.

"Uh, so what did you find out? Gerry is my boss and he doesn't like me very much," asked Colt.

"Well, you guys run a simple mail system with almost no security. But, it has a log of who does what. I went in and looked at your account. It got messed with by someone with admin access. It was that Gerry guy."

"So what can he do with my account?"

"He can log in with another account and send emails but it looks like it's coming from you."

"Crap. What can I do? Who knows what kind of bogus crap he might send out?" whined Colt.

"You could get another email account. But, I guess he could do the same thing. And, since he's your boss, he would know if you tried to get around what he's doing."

"Dude, can you track this stuff? I don't have a good feeling about this," asked Colt.

Fletcher thought about his project and wondered how much he should tell them about his capabilities. Since he expected to be gone in a few months, he relaxed.

"Uh, I can track whatever he does. I'll set something up," said Fletcher.

Colt sensed that Fletcher would be happy if he and Bobby left now. However, he saw this as an opportunity to see what Fletcher was working on in secret. Also, the pizza wasn't touched.

"Hey, let's eat some of this pizza," said Colt.

After eating for awhile, in silence, Bobby surprised the other two by opening the conversation.

"Hey man. What do you do with all of this equipment?" he asked.

"Uh, I've been working on a upgrade to a system that can interrogate the network and push out stuff to PCs," answered Fletcher.

"Wow, that sounds radical. What company is it for?" asked Colt.

Fletcher froze. *I've never said anything to anybody until now.*

182

"I'll just say that it's a not a company you would have heard of. And, I'm almost done. That's all I can say."

Colt looked at Bobby and smiled.

Later, as they walked toward their dorm room, Colt put his arm on Bobby's shoulder.

"I bet that nerd is working on some Microsoft thing. And, I bet he'll get a lot of money, stock or whatever when he's done. Dude, we better stay friends with Fletcher."

"No one would believe it. And he's doing it on the campus network, too," said Bobby.

Chapter 37

From: Strong, Amy[AmyStrong@WWU.edu]
To: Bower, Suzy[susybower@EWU.edu]
Subject: What should I do?

Hey Suzy
I know it just happened but I wonder what I should do? Should I
tell Colt. It may be nothing. Help#####

Amy

Colt was again sitting in Gerry' office. It was lunchtime and
rain was pelting the windows. It reminded him of his visits to
his father's den at home. Until recently nothing good had
happened in that room. As always the huge, nerdy, stubborn
man sat behind his desk staring at Colt. *Well at least he doesn't seem
to be pissed at me*, thought Colt. *I better just keep my mouth shut
anyway. You never know with this guy.*

Gerry removed his gaze and looked down at some papers
sitting on his desk. Colt thought about every previous meeting
with Gerry as well as whatever dreams he had that related to his
boss. He tried to read his mood and couldn't sense anything
negative but still felt uneasy. After a few minutes Gerry looked
up and spoke.

"I know we've had our differences but lately I'm seeing improvements in your work and attitude. I just wanted to say that I think you're on the right track," said Gerry.

At the same time that Colt smiled inside, he felt like he had been jabbed in his right side by a crowbar. His happiness at being recognized and the hope for a better relationship with his boss disappeared as he looked for someone with a pointed object next to him. He saw nothing but was now on the defensive. *It must be my psychic abilities warning me.*

"Uh, uh, thanks Gerry. I've been trying to improve," said Colt.

"You know, I'm here to help you in any way I can. We both want the work to get done and to have success."

Colt thought about different times Gerry had tried to sabotage his efforts and especially the recent meeting where he didn't support him at all. *I wonder what Mr. Carbon would tell me to say, now? I'm really sure it's not what I want to say.*

"Well, it helps that Bobby Jones is working with me. We can almost keep up with the tickets now. Is that all you wanted to talk about?" asked Colt.

Colt thought he saw a frown on Gerry's face at the mention of Bobby's name. Getting the okay for Bobby to help him was one of Colt's greatest accomplishments. After extreme resistance, Gerry had to give in when his boss insisted. Of course, the stubborn anti-Windows manager acted like it was his decision.

"Uh,…that's good. That's all I had. Just keep up the good work."

"Thanks," answered Colt who exited as quickly as possible.

Once the door was closed, Gerry grabbed the papers on his desk and crumpled them up.

"Fuck that little twerp," he yelled as he threw the paper ball at the door.

As Colt walked back to his dorm room he thought, *there's something up with old Gerry the genie. I can feel it.*

Once Colt was back in his room he tried to relax before turning on his pager to receive tickets. He still wondered about the meeting with his boss but soon tired of thinking about it. His cell phone rang. It was Amy.

"Hi sweetie. What's up?"

"I just wanted to call to see how your day has been," she said.

"Well I had a meeting with Gerry. It was very weird. Now he's being nice to me."

"Maybe that's good. You're doing great at your job. Everybody's noticing."

"I just don't trust that dude. So what else is goin' on?" asked Colt.

After no answer Colt felt the need to fill in the emptiness with some words.

"Uh, is everything okay?" he asked.

"Oh uh, yeah. I was just thinking. Everything's fine. Let's get together after your work. Okay?"

"Sure, I'll call you when I get off."

"Bye"

"Bye"

Colt closed his eyes and pictured a mountainous region with a flat plain. It reminded him of his vision of the yogi in the cave. It felt like he was very high up in the sky. Then his thoughts about Gerry and Amy began to coalesce into feelings of foreboding. As he grappled with dark emotions, he saw the sky change over one of the lower mountain tops. He noticed a faint brownish color. In what seemed like seconds. Colt was being bombarded by a sandstorm. Although it was all internal, he felt like his entire body was being sandpapered. He tried to grab the small table next to the chair he was sitting in while opening his eyes. His hand hit the corner of the table and he landed on the floor on his chin making him more disoriented than he already was. He fought with the image of the sandstorm overlaid onto his small dorm room for some time. Finally he was able to pull himself back into waking reality by touching his hand to the base of his spine and focusing on a lamp sitting near him.

After making some coffee and working on his computer for a short time, he felt that he was okay to start work. The vision of the storm lingered but he couldn't decide what it was related to. He turned on his pager which started beeping at him at once. *I guess I better get going. But what the hell was that storm all about? It can't be good. And just when I thought things would start to get easy.*

Chapter 38

------Email-------
From: Lathrop, Gerry[GerryLathrop@WWU.edu]
To: Snow, Robert[RSnow@WWU.edu]
Subject: Colt O'Brien

Hi Bob
I have seen improvements in Colt O'Brien's work habits. But, I am still having a difficult time fully trusting him. I guess it will take some time. I will wait to decide about his future but I am sensing a hidden agenda. As you know, his helper is Bobby Jones who just went through rehab. I am also watching him very closely.
Gerry

------Email-------

Bobby sat in the dark dorm room at 3 am in the morning. Colt slept soundly as evidenced by his steady breathing. Sweat poured down Bobby's face causing his eyes to sting. Although he could not see them, his hands were shaking. *Fuck this recovery shit. One drink won't hurt. I just need to feel right again. Then everything will be okay.* He thought about the effort it would take to track down some alcohol since there wasn't any in their room. Then, he realized that he didn't have any money to spend. As he started to wonder where Colt's money was he stopped himself from embarking on a journey that he knew would be filled with pain and guilt. *I guess I better go to a meeting when I can. Is this thing ever going to let go of me?*

Colt woke and knew that he had slept for a long time and deeply. He knew because he couldn't remember his dreams and he felt more rested than he had in months. He attempted to overcome his lack of interest in classes or anything else that entailed effort with little success. He smelled rich coffee fumes floating out of the small kitchen and smiled. Bobby sat in a chair drinking coffee.

"Hey Colt, it's getting a little late. Don't you have class?" asked Bobby.

"Uh, uh, whatever. I need some of that coffee before I answer questions," answered Colt.

"You looked so happy sleeping that I let you sleep. I guessed that you needed it."

Colt got a large mug of coffee and sat in the other chair facing Bobby. He quickly downed some of the jet black liquid. It was strong and he started to wake up. He noticed that his friend looked pale and drawn.

"Dude, are you okay?"

"I woke up early and wanted a drink. But, I'm okay now. I'll be going to a meeting later. Man, this shit is bad news. Just when I think it's no big deal, I go berserk with cravings."

"I'm glad I talked to your counselor. I can see how bad it is now. I had no idea. He said you would have days like this in the beginning," said Colt.

"I'll tell you this. Addiction can make you do really bad things. It's like you forget about what's right and just do stuff. And people get hurt."

"You go to that meeting. You're doing great so far. Everybody thinks so. I know it's hard but you won't last long if you go back to where you were."

"Yeah, I'm lucky I have support. So, is anything going on with you?

"I've been so busy that Amy and I are like strangers. I think she wants to talk but is avoiding something."

"Man, she's the best thing that ever happened to you. You better deal with it."

"Oh I know that I lucked out. I'll give her a little more time and ask her what's up.

After a few cups of coffee, Colt was contemplating taking a shower and doing something. He knew that in a few hours he would be working trouble tickets. *Maybe I'll just take it easy until work. I can catch up on the class stuff later.*

In no time at all Colt was showered and sitting in front of his computer. Bobby sat at his laptop which was connected by a wire to a small device on the floor. Both of them were screaming as they played a computer game named "Descent 2 Vertigo". Although there was no sound from Bobby's laptop, booming electronic music played out of the speakers attached to Colt's tower computer. Both of them were engrossed in the game.

There was a break in the music and Colt heard his cell phone ringing. He reluctantly answered after pausing the game. Bobby groaned.

"You stopped because I was kicking your ass," he said.

"Hey Bobinator. You just keep telling yourself that but remember that it's a dream. I had your ass," answered Colt.

Colt looked at his phone and answered.

"Hey dude. What's up?" said Colt.

"Uh yeah. Er. uh," said a tentative voice.

"Spit it out Fletcher," said Colt.

"Umm. Well I saw some more weird stuff on your email account. A whole bunch of emails got sent out from you. I don't think you did it though," said Fletcher.

"Wait a minute. I don't send out that much email. How many were sent?" asked Colt.

"About a hundred in about an hour."

"No way I did that."

"I redirected one. I'll read it to you. The subject is 'critical notice'."

"What the hell," yelled Colt.

"The email says to click on the link below."

"Where does the link go to?" asked Colt.

"It goes to some weird site that sells T-shirts but that's not all."

"I don't know if I want to hear the rest. It can't be good." said Colt.

"As soon as I got to the site about 20 pop-up windows hit the screen. Each one was a different web site. Some were to sites with naked girls. I couldn't get rid of the pop-ups without rebooting."

"Have you figured out who did this?" asked Colt.

"Uh, er, it wasn't as easy as before. I'm still working on it.?

"Hey dude. Thanks. I'll do a little investigation myself."

"Yeah, seeya later," said Fletcher.

Colt leaned back. His mind was racing. He thought of Gerry and knew that he was behind this latest attempt to make his life difficult, if not impossible. Just when he was ready to call Gerry to have a meeting, his pager started beeping.

Oh no. I didn't even think about trouble tickets. Here we go.

Chapter 39

------Email-------
From: Boyd, Allen[AllenBoyd@norton.com]
To: Oleson, Sven[SOleson@mcaffee.com]
Subject: This is a bad one.

Hey Sven

This latest virus is really causing a lot of problems. Let's work together to find a fix. This is a nasty one.

Allen

------Email-------

Amy was on the phone with Suzy Bower. It was not a pleasant conversation for Amy with Suzy telling her what she should do.

"I don't know if I'm ready to tell him anything yet. Don't you think it's too soon?" asked Amy.

"Listen, I warned you about how easy it is to end up in this situation. Now you need to at least be honest about it. Colt will understand," said Suzy.

"But he's already under a lot of pressure with his job and everything. I don't want to give him more stuff to deal with. And, it may be nothing."

"I don't want to hear another word. Call him as soon as I hang up. Bye."

The silent void enveloped Amy like a dark, ominous cloud. In spite of her urge to run and hide, she forced herself to dial Colt's number. He answered immediately.

"Hey, what's up? I can't talk long. We have another emergency."

"Oh I just wanted to talk but it can wait," said Amy.

"I've been thinking that you had something to talk about. Will it take long?" asked Colt.

"Oh, uh, if you're busy I don't want to do it now. When you have some time let's sit down and talk about it."

"Uh okay. Sorry but I have to go. See ya later."

"Bye," said Amy with a sigh of relief.

As soon as he realized that this new attack on Windows computers would generate numerous trouble tickets, Colt's mind went into another gear. He knew from experience that he would need razor-like focus and a reserve of energy to deal with the threat. After assessing the situation with Bobby at his side, Colt knew this would be very messy. The virus not only caused multiple web sites to pop up forcing the user to reboot but it also sent out emails to everyone on the user's contact list. Not only was it affecting university computers but also machines outside the campus network. Colt decided he needed help and called a meeting back at his dorm room with Bobby and Fletcher. He also invited Billy Carbon to participate by telephone.

"You're on speaker said Colt to Billy. Bobby Jones, and Fletcher Rowe are with me," said Colt.

"Uh, who, really, Fletcher Rowe?" asked Billy.

"Uh yeah. Didn't you meet him at my party? Fletcher helped us with the last virus we had," said Colt.

"Uh, I guess I didn't meet him yet. Er, uh, er, there's a Fletcher Rowe that is like an internet legend. He's an expert on network analysis and stuff. Is it the same guy? We weren't sure he was a real person," asked Billy.

Fletcher who was fidgeting in his lawn chair looked like he had been hiding in a cubby hole and someone opened the door.

"Hey don't worry about that right now. We need to get this virus fixed," said Fletcher.

Billy paused causing everyone to wonder about the mysterious Fletcher and his internet reputation. *What is this guy doing at Western*, thought Bobby?

"Well, Gunnar is here with me. We both looked around and couldn't find much on the virus. It looks like some hackers in Europe put it out there. Some groups are working on a fix but nothing yet," said Billy.

"Crap, I can't believe we have another virus. This is going to be a shit storm. I guess we can try to see what we can do ourselves while we wait for a fix."

"Yeah, we have a test machine. We were able to get rid of the thing by booting with a DOS disk and deleting the email folder. But, we lost all of our emails, contacts and other junk in there. Maybe you guys can do better." said Billy.

"Yeah, losing all those emails will really piss people off. I guess we better get to work. We have about a million tickets. See ya later. Thanks," said Colt.

After Billy hung up, Fletcher made some suggestions and said he would research a better way to clean the virus. As he headed toward the door, Fletcher turned to Colt.

"Oh, I forgot. I can't tell for sure but I think it's that guy Gerry again who did this. I doubt that anybody else has admin rights."

"I figured it was him anyway. Maybe you can keep looking so we can prove he did it. This is really starting to piss me off."

Colt knew that he and Bobby couldn't wait. They grabbed their tool kits and started working in their own building. They decided that having a plan of attack, no matter how inefficient was better than doing nothing. Colt had a feeling of dread but Bobby was happy to be occupied. He was able to forget about his desire to have just one drink.

With each person they helped Colt presented two options. Option one was to leave the computer turned off and wait for a fix to be found. Option two was to do as Billy suggested but lose all current and saved emails. If they chose option two, Colt and Bobby would re-install email on their machine. Most people could not see themselves without a computer for very long and chose option two. Colt and Bobby split up after fixing a few computers. They found that the recovery process took about 30 minutes for each machine.

After a few hours Colt's cell phone rang. He saw that it was Gerry and answered.

"Where are you Colt?" asked Gerry in a nonchalant way.

"Bobby and I are working tickets in our dorm building," answered Colt.

"Uh okay, I'm just checking. This virus sounds like a bad one?"

"Uh yeah, it is but we're fixing some PCs," answered Colt.

"That's all I need. Oh, what room are you in?"

"Uh, room 304."

"Bye," said Gerry.

Something from deep inside Colt's mind nudged him. He tried to process the conversation but knew he was forgetting something. *Crap, what is it? What am I missing? If I wasn't so busy, maybe I could figure it out.*

Just as he was grabbing on to the tidbit of information, he was trying to remember, the door to the dorm room flew open. Two burly campus security personnel briskly walked in and grabbed his arms. Both were thick and strong. The one with reddish hair spoke.

"Are you Colt O'Brien?"

Only then did Colt understand what his mind was trying to process just a minute earlier. *It was my account that sent those emails!*

Chapter 40

------**Email**-------
From: Rowe, Fletcher[FRow@topmail.org]
To: Freeman, John[freebird@anonymous.org]
Subject: Help

Hey John
I need some help with an email hack I am investigating. This
guy is getting set up and I need to prove that he is innocent.
Let me know if you or some of the team can give me a hand.

Fletcher

------**Email**-------

Colt and Bobby were trying to avoid the herd of criminal types and miscreants in the holding cell at the Bellingham police station. The group changed as individuals came and went but the general appearance and mentality remained the same. Neither of them was intimidated by the scraggly looking group that surrounded them. However, they didn't want trouble and hoped to be out of jail soon.

"Man, when do we get out of here?" whispered Bobby.

"I can't believe that asshole Gerry went this far. But, we didn't do anything. How can they keep us locked up with these lowlifes?" said Colt.

Bobby looked around trying to gauge the mood of the mostly young men of color that populated the holding cell.

"So far nobody has given us any trouble? Do you think these guys will try to push us around?" asked Bobby.

"Let's just keep quiet and hope this doesn't last long. I don't know how it works in here. I guess anything can happen."

A policeman opened the door to the cell and pointed to Colt and Bobby. They followed him to an interrogation room and sat facing a 30ish, sharply dressed man. He had sandy brown hair. *This guy has to be FBI,* thought Colt. *This can't be good.*

"Hello guys. I'm Art Stone. I want to help you get out of this mess. Hell, not that long ago I was young and stupid. I can relate."

"Wow, someone to help us. Man, am I glad to see you," said Bobby.

Colt used his inner psychic ability to check out what Art Stone's agenda was and put his hand on Bobby's arm. He looked at him as if to say 'watch out'.

"So how do we get out of here?" asked Colt.

"I know you guys were probably just showing off your computer skills and it got out of hand. A simple statement will clear everything up," said Art with a warm smile.

"Hey dude. Here's our statement. We didn't do anything. I think it was Gerry," said Colt.

"Oh, you mean your boss Gerry? The guy who gave us a history of your work performance and turned you in? You mean the responsible adult in this situation?"

"Screw that. I never sent that email. Even if I wanted to do something like that, I'm not that stupid. Can't you see that I'm being set up?" yelled Colt.

"Listen to me, you little twerp. This is a federal crime. And, the more you lie, the worse it will get. Right now half the computers on your campus are down and the thing has spread all over the place," blurted Art showing that a bit of anger lurked under the soft veneer.

"Yeah, well maybe Gerry was in such a hurry to make me look bad that he screwed things up more than he wanted to. Go talk to him," said Colt.

Bobby was taken to another room for separate questioning while Colt remained with Art the FBI guy. After hours of interrogation they both were again in the holding cell.

"So what happened with you? Why did they put us in different rooms?" asked Bobby.

"They probably wanted to see if our stories stayed the same. You know, like on TV shows. I can't believe he thought I was going to change my mind and confess. What an idiot," answered Colt.

After only a few minutes two scruffy looking guys approached them. Colt guessed they were in their twenties but they seemed older due to a worn out look and bad teeth. One was skinny with long brown hair and about Bobby's height. He wore a black t-shirt that had the words 'Feed on Speed' across the front in white. The other was also skinny but much shorter. He had a scar across his forehead and was sporting a crew cut. *Uh oh, here comes two losers*, thought Colt. In his mind he named them Stringy and Baldy. Bobby looked up and tensed as the two lowlifes invaded his space.

"Hey pussy, what are you in for?" asked Stringy.

Colt first noticed that they smelled like they hadn't had a bath in weeks. He sensed that they were looking for trouble and somehow knew that they didn't need a reason to be violent. He didn't want trouble but wasn't about to be pushed around by weak looking druggies. Although he was not generally a fearful person this situation caught Bobby off guard. He was speechless and hoped that Colt would take charge like he usually did. Colt tried to calm his mind before answering.

"We just had a misunderstanding. We'll be out soon. What about you guys?"

Little Baldy started pulling on Bobby's shirt and nudging him gently. The other hoodlum spoke.

"Don't fuckin' worry about why we're in here. We can't be fucked with, even in here. Do you want to fuck with us college boy?"

Colt tensed and prepared for physical interaction but had no fear of these two. He saw that Bobby was very uncomfortable but felt confident that he could handle the two uninvited guests alone *Just a coupla loudmouths. Probably are coming down from some drug.* He looked Stringy directly in the eyes and radiated confidence mixed in with a little irritation.

"Listen asshole. Nobody is messing with you but if you don't get away from us now, shit will happen."

Now Colt's legs were spread slightly and his knees were bent. He looked at Bobby who now seemed resigned to Colt's approach of dealing with the situation head on. He flashed his arm at Baldy's hand, which was holding on to his shirt. The much shorter man backed up slightly.

Baldy's partner swung at Colt's nose but missed as Colt easily pushed his arm to the side. Colt stood his ground as Bobby backed into him. Baldy punched his stomach taking his breath away. Then, both attackers threw themselves into Colt and Bobby. Colt decided to end this and punched his assailant in the nose with one fist and his side with the other. The effect was immediate and stopped Stringy in his tracks. He bent over and held his nose as Colt brought his knee into his head. Bobby was surprised by the viciousness of his attacker and struggled to hold his ground. Just as he felt like he was on solid footing and able to fend of Baldy's attack, he felt an intense flash of pain as Baldy's fist hit him on the forehead. Next, he felt the back of his head bang into something. Something deep inside Bobby woke up and he became like a crazy man. He turned on his attacker with all of his strength. Baldy was overwhelmed by Bobby's determination and hatred and ended up bloody on the concrete floor. As Baldy crawled away and his partner followed, Bobby saw a policeman enter the cell.

He asked, "What's going on here?" to no one in particular.

"Those guys jumped us. We didn't do anything," said Bobby.

"What about him?" asked the officer with a look of concern.

Bobby turned to see Colt lying on the floor. He was not moving. His eyes were wide open but lifeless. He appeared to be dead.

Chapter 41

------Email-------
From: Anonymous, Mr.[mranon@anonymous.net]
To: Snow, Robert[RSnow@wwu.edu]
Subject: Virus attack. It wasn't Colt

Hi Robert

I am a person with special computing skills and friends who also have such skills. It has come to my attention that Colt O'Brien has been arrested in connection with a virus event on the WWU campus. I can't tell you how but I know that he is not responsible. The guilty party is someone named Gerry. If you don't believe me there is an easy way to prove that what I am saying is true. I hope that you take the time to investigate this situation. An innocent student's career and reputation are at stake. Please consider following my suggestions below.......

------Email-------

Gerry sat at his desk with no regrets. The virus was still out of control and his UNIX technologists were having a difficult time dealing with it, but his primary goal had been achieved. He smiled as he pictured Colt and Bobby sitting in a jail cell and answering pointed questions about their involvement. He made sure that the FBI received incriminating information for their investigation. He saw no way that Colt could prove his innocence. Gerry's desk phone rang and he answered.

"Hi Gerry. How goes the battle?" asked his boss Robert Snow.

Gerry wondered what Robert wanted. The virus was causing problems everywhere but he knew that the blame was right where he wanted it to be.

"Well, that little twerp really screwed things up. It's going to take awhile for us to get things sorted out. I just hope he didn't screw other things up that we don't know about, too," answered Gerry.

"I just have to wonder why Colt and his friend did something like that? It seems so pointless," mused Robert.

"I told you that he was a loose cannon. I know he seemed like a nice kid but I always had my doubts."

"You know that Colt denies doing this. I've been talking to an outside consultant who seems to know his stuff. He will be doing a separate investigation. He will need access to our systems," said Robert.

"Uh, okay. Why are you doing that?"

"Well, we don't want to appear biased. There could be a lawsuit or something. Both the kid's parents have been on the phone with me. And, a guy named Matthew Carbon called. They seem very serious about pursuing legal action."

"As far as I can tell the facts prove that Colt did it. I think that his drinking buddy probably helped," said Gerry.

"At any rate, the guy who will investigate told me that from now on we need to be sure that no one touches Colt's or Bobby's email information on their laptops or the server. He said something about a history log. He'll be up here in a few days after he finishes up on a project he's working on."

"Yeah, I'll make sure that nobody touches anything," said Gerry.

"Thanks Gerry. Now that my email is working again, I will send you the consultant's information. I'll say this. I sure feel for the people that still don't have email. Thanks" said Robert.

"Thank you," said Gerry.

Gerry sat in his chair stunned. It was as if someone hit him in the face when he was expecting a hug of gratitude. *Shit, I better do something fast. If this outside guy is any good, he might be able to uncover what I did.* Gerry immediately locked the door to his office and told his secretary that he would be unavailable for an hour. After logging on he quickly accessed the mail server and found the log file that tracked email activities. After searching for and finding entries for Colt's account he deleted a few items and logged off of the system. Gerry raised his arms and smiled. *Well, that takes care of that. The last little thing to finish off Colt O'Brien,* he thought.

~~~

When Colt was hit on the back of his skull by Bobby's head, he was instantly knocked out. He found himself looking down on Bobby and the police officer who were staring down at his own body. After a short period of adjustment to this new situation, he felt a strong pull. Although he wanted to yell at his friend to tell him that he was okay, Colt gave in to the overwhelming current that was drawing him away. As he floated away from the jail cell he thought *here I go again.* He guessed that he was approaching familiar territory. However, this time turned out to be different. He seemed to be able to think in a logical manner and the emotional turmoil of his previous out of body experience was non-existent. The further he traveled the more he seemed to be going in the correct direction toward the right destination. He did nothing to make this happen. He only observed and tried to feel what was happening. Over time, which to him seemed to be not functioning normally, he was overcome with feelings of peace, happiness and unworldly confidence. He sensed that, in this place, he was untouchable by anything or anyone. Although it made little difference to him, he thought *maybe I'm dead and I'm headed toward heaven.*

Gradually Colt saw and was enveloped by a soft white light that appeared out of nowhere. He knew it was spiritual because he felt the presence of a higher being. The ability of his mind to think and speak in words was limited. Those abilities were replaced by a different and more subtle form of communication. Although he saw nothing but white, penetrating light, he felt the presence of a personal entity. It was if he had merged with a spark of infinity but with a personality. As Colt adjusted to this new way of experiencing he absorbed the communication that was being transmitted into his soul. It was communicated to him that it was not his time to die and that his spiritual growth would take place on the Earth for some time. He also was shown, in an instant, the pitfalls of using his special psychic abilities without understanding what was happening. In the state that Colt was in, he didn't care about anything earthly or if he lived or died. He knew that life was eternal. He knew that nothing could harm his real self now or ever. The situation with the virus and his boss Gerry was presented to him with a cause and an outcome. It made perfect sense to Colt. He saw himself as an inexperienced sleeper who made decisions based on little valid information. Then he saw Amy and knew why he was to live and not move on to the next thing. She held a naked baby, wrapped in a blue blanket, snugly in her arms. It was sleeping. For some reason he noticed the delicate, fuzzy hair on the infant's almost bald head. Although he didn't think that he could feel happier than he was, a wave of pure love washed over him at the sight of the child.

As suddenly as Colt had left his body, he was slapped back into it. He plummeted out of his serene, painless, spiritual state and into a body that was still feeling the effects of his ordeal. Harsh reality assailed him. He felt like his head was a reverberating bell. His entry into the world of the living was so abrupt that he could not find his bearings and was overcome with dizziness. He felt a hand on his arm and was able to look up at Amy. Fear animated her face. He knew that others were also in the room but saw only her. Through a haze of confusion and dizziness he used all of his willpower to focus on Amy.

When her eyes connected with his he said, "It's going to be a boy."

Chapter 42

------**Email**-------
From: O'Brien, Colt[ColtOB@WWU.edu]
To: Carbon, Matthew[MatthewC@hocs.biz]
Subject: Can we talk?

Hi Mr. Carbon
Things seemed to have worked out around here. Much thanks to you and your wife for good solid advice. I would like to come over and thank you in person also. And I may have some other news by then.
Colt

------**Email**-------

Gerry sat in an interrogation room across from Art Stone. The FBI officer had been caught off guard when they nabbed Gerry in the middle of his cover-up of the evidence. Usually it was the young hackers, trying to show off, who perpetrated this type of computer crime. However odd it seemed, there was no doubt that Gerry was guilty. Once they knew what to look for, uncovering the truth was simple. The note from the anonymous source told them where to look for the damning data. They found it before Robert Snow called Gerry. The last thing they needed was to see him in the act of covering up the crime. When Gerry logged onto the system to erase evidence, FBI computer specialists were watching. He had no sooner logged off than he was hauled in.

They had been at it for a few hours and Gerry was becoming agitated. In the beginning he had denied everything. However the evidence placed in front of Gerry was rock solid. After Mr.

Stone asked and re-asked subtle and direct questions, Gerry's sense of safety lessened. Now he was bright red and was breathing rapidly. Art Stone was concerned that he might faint from hyperventilating.

"Hey Gerry. Try to calm down a little. I'm becoming concerned," said Art.

"Yeah, well I can't help it. You keep twisting what I say around," cried Gerry.

"That's because it doesn't make sense. Listen, I think I can make this easier on you if you come clean. I really don't think you wanted it to go this far. Right now if you are convicted it could be some serious jail time. But, if you tell us what happened, I expect it won't be too bad."

Gerry looked at Art with fear. Sweat poured down his face. Although he tried, he could not stop shaking.

"I want a lawyer. I have rights," said Gerry.

"Here's the deal. We have all the evidence we need. If you don't help us out here and save the taxpayers some money, we will come at you hard. If you get a lawyer, he's going to advise you to cut a deal. But the deal won't be as good if you waste our time."

"I'll see what my lawyer says."

"I suggest you think about it. We can play ball if you want to. I hope you wake up and cut the deal," said Art with a pleasant smile.

~~~

Both Colt and Bobby were released as soon as it was obvious that Gerry was behind the virus attack. In the end, they were locked up for three days. Colt was in the hospital at the time of the release. Bobby was ecstatic the moment he strolled out of the Bellingham jail. Even the sun was shining which seemed appropriate to him. Although Colt had a serious concussion, he recovered quickly and was released a few days later. His doctor was surprised that Colt's symptoms disappeared so fast. He even allowed him to go back to work. Much like the earlier virus attack, a fix was created and Fletcher wrote the software needed to repair the computers on the school network. Colt and Bobby applied the fix to computers that were not on the network over a period of about a week. Colt and Amy were together more but a widening gap was forming between then. She still avoided talking about her condition which had been verified by a simple at home test. When Colt had come out of his coma joy gushed up from her heart. But when he indicated that he knew about the baby, she became nervous and unsure of herself. In the past she generally felt steady and in control but now life seemed dangerous and unpredictable. Her lack of confidence led to a routine of avoiding life in general and closeness to Colt in particular. She needed to sort things out and decide what she wanted to do. While Colt recovered, he tried to not put any pressure on Amy. He never felt that their relationship was in jeopardy and was willing to be patient.

Colt was changed from his near-death experience and saw his life as an unending wonder made up of a simple series of steps. Unlike in his previous psychic experiences he did not forget any of what happened while he was in the light and feeling the presence of a personal guide. It still permeated his being with each waking minute. He felt like he had a purpose and that everything would work out as long as he was true to the highest ideals and did his best. Amy would be his first priority but he could see that she wasn't ready to open up about her pregnancy or their future. He remained busy adjusting to his new way of seeing things as well as finishing up the work he was doing on the virus attack. He hoped that by continuing to help with trouble tickets, his reputation would be improved after all of the confusing and misleading information about him.

When the computer work was finished, Colt again created a report. It was similar to the one he used for his presentation when defending himself after the first virus attack. However, this time he only presented his data to Robert Snow, who had stepped in when Gerry was arrested. Robert did not micro-manage as Gerry was apt to do, which gave Colt the feeling that he was supported and trusted. Sitting in front of the intelligent, pleasant manager was radically different from similar meetings with Gerry. Colt went over the steps taken to fix the virus problem and presented a summary of the number of computers affected, man hours, etc.

"So it took us almost three weeks of work. Of course we were interrupted at the beginning," said Colt.

"Colt, you've done a fantastic job. Bobby too," said Robert Snow.

"I just need to know that I won't have any more problems with being accused of stuff I didn't do," said Colt.

"You are in the clear. Gerry confessed to everything after he saw that it was in his best interests. I know that your reputation took a hit but I'll try to help you with that."

"Thanks. I appreciate it," said Colt with a smile.

"I expect you will have lots of opportunities to show people the great work you do. Over time, nobody will remember the bad rumors. I know you will show everybody what a great worker you are."

"Yeah, if I stay in this job," said Colt.

"Well, I know this has been tough but I hope you aren't considering leaving. We need you," said Robert.

"You never know what will happen." said Colt.

"By the way, I'm still wondering who sent that email to me. His or her plan to catch Gerry worked. Do you know who it might be?"

"Uh, er, uh, I don't know but I sure am glad someone likes me."

~~~

Colt and Bobby sat in Starbucks in Bellingham. Fletcher Rowe sat across from them. Fletcher seemed less out of place than usual but still Colt wondered about his ability to function outside of his computer-filled dorm room. Bobby put a paper bag on the table. Fletcher looked up and spoke.

"Wow Colt, a lot has happened to you. I'm sure glad you came out of it okay. Bobby and I want to thank you for supporting us and giving us a chance. I know that I feel more a part of things than before."

"Yeah, me too. I really needed a friend when I was not being a stupid ass. Thanks," said Bobby.

"C'mon, it's no big deal. Dudes, you helped me. No way I could have fixed all those problems without you guys. I always felt that you two would do anything for me," answered Colt.

"We got you something. Look in the bag," said Bobby.

Colt pulled out three baseball style caps. One was purple, one was bright red and the other was day-glo orange. Each of them had the words 'Computer Hero' sewn onto the front.

"Thanks. I think these will go nicely with my wardrobe," said Colt with a big grin.

Chapter 43

```
------Email-------
From: O'Brien, Colt[ColtOB@WWU.edu]
To: O'Brien, Kelly[Kellyobrien@UW.edu]
Subject: Family
-----------------------------------------------------------------------
```

hey kel
big things are coming. I can't tell you any more right now

your bro

```
------Email-------
```

Colt could see the end of the school year in sight. It hadn't gone as he expected, not even close. *I wonder if life is going to always be different from what I expect?* It seemed that not one part of going to college was easy. Although Colt expected Gerry to be difficult, he underestimated his deviousness. *I guess seeing stuff and feeling stuff doesn't stop bad things from happening,* he thought. More than ever Colt believed that doing things alone was not a good approach for success. He appreciated the help he received as he tried to survive different kinds of challenge. He thought about how Mr. and Mrs. Carbon were especially helpful and asked nothing in return. One saved his life and the other might have saved his career. As he remembered and took into account what he had learned, the most intense lessons had been due to his experimentation with his psychic abilities. *Even though I had the right intentions, I didn't know what the hell I was doing. Man, did I find out how weird and painful that out of body stuff can get.* In the end, after everything that happened, he felt like he'd found himself and had direction. His interest in using psychic abilities, for anything, was taking a back seat to just doing the daily tasks put before him. The result of his near-death experience was that he had a new outlook on everything. Although he was not brought up in a religious household, he sensed that he had touched something spiritual. The experience had opened a new way of thinking for him. It was an eternal feeling that felt beyond all of his dreams, psychic experiences and feelings. *I'm going to find out where this spiritual thing leads me. If that's what it is. I know it might disappear but it feels like something that lasts forever.* For Colt, the world and everything in it, had changed. Although he had come out of his trials in good shape and would have good grades, a good reputation and enhanced computer skills, he still had one part of his life to deal with. *I really, really need to have that talk with Amy.*

~ ~ ~

Now that things had settled down, Colt had approached Amy about having a talk. She was not receptive and avoided his many advances. Since Colt had been recovering he let it slide but now he was starting to become concerned. Instead of calling, he went to her dorm room when he thought she might be there. As Amy opened the door she went pale and said nothing. Colt looked at her with his nicest smile.

"We need to talk. Can I come in?" asked Colt.

Amy's eyes reflected frustration, slight anger, and most of all fear.

"Now is not a good time. I'm really busy."

"Come on Amy. You keep shutting me out. Just give me five minutes."

"I don't know if I'm ready to talk yet."

"What? I can't believe this. Are you breaking up with me?" yelled Colt.

"Listen, let's meet here in a few days."

Colt had gone from slight nervousness to anger and then consternation in a matter of minutes. *What the hell is this*, he thought.

"Okay, in a few days then. Call me when you have a day and time."

Colt turned and left. Pools of tears formed in Amy's eyes and spilled over rolling down her reddened cheeks.

Colt sat in his dorm room trying to figure out what just happened. *Goddamn women. Just when you think you know what the hell is going on, they flip out. Maybe if I talk to Kelly, she can help me.*

Colt was surprised again when Amy sent him an email instead of calling. Finally the day of the meeting came. Colt thought about Amy as he walked to her dorm room. Unlike in so many young romances, Colt felt deeper in love than ever. Rather than losing interest and seeing things not to like, he respected and adored her more with each day. *No way I'm letting her go. No way.*

After letting Colt in they sat on opposite ends of the small dorm room. Again Amy seemed out of sorts to Colt who only wanted everything to be okay.

"Listen, whatever problems we have, we can work it out. I have something to ask you," said Colt.

Amy pushed her chin out while the rest of her body tensed, like a huge rope that was twisted much too tightly. To Colt it seemed like she was ready to explode. He had never seen her like this and decided to try not to push too hard. Amy pointed her finger at Colt with fierce, sparkling eyes.

"No, you listen to me. I've decided some things for myself. And, I don't care what you or anybody else says," spit out Amy.

Colt could feel a wall of hot emotional energy coming at him but he still didn't know why. This was not an Amy he had ever seen. Colt spoke softly.

"What have you decided?"

"Everybody thinks I need to follow the plan. I was supposed to finish school. I was supposed to get a job and all of that. Well I don't give a shit what everybody else thinks. I'm having my baby. I'm having my baby."

In a flash of understanding, Colt realized that he never considered that there was a question about Amy having their child. He had seen it. He was directed to live so that he could be a father and husband. To him it was all decided and obvious. Now he saw that Amy knew almost nothing about how he felt. She was fighting for her life and that of her unborn baby. Most of all she felt alone. *Oh, I've been so stupid. So,so stupid.*

Amy burst into tears as Colt rushed to her. He held her in his arms and started to cry himself.

"I want that too Amy. I want you to have our son," said Colt.

Amy grabbed onto Colt like a tightened vise and looked into his face with hope.

"Do you really mean that?" she asked.

"Will you marry me? Will you be my wife?" asked Colt.

"Oh yes! Oh yes I will," she sobbed through a cascade of tears.

Chapter 44

Wow girl
I just got off the phone with my brother. Im still dizzy
from all the news. First he tells me that you're pregnant
and then he says you two are getting married. It's almost
more than I can handle. I have so many questions I don't
know where to start. Let's talk when school is out next
month. Oh and congratulations.
Kelly

------Email-------

Gerry Lathrop was halfway through his one year prison
sentence. After the year was up he would finish out his time by
doing community service for another eighteen months. After a
few months of adjusting to a new routine while imprisoned, he
saw an opportunity to do something to keep his restless mind
occupied. It was brought to his attention that inmates were
allowed to teach computer classes if they stayed out of trouble
and had the appropriate background. He now sat in front of the
warden, Davis Harding. The pleasant, thin man with sharp facial
features and receding hairline, smiled back at Gerry.

"So, I think I would make a good teacher for these guys. I
have a lot of experience as you know," said Gerry with
confidence.

"Gerry, you have been a good inmate. I think your idea has merit. So, do you have an idea of what kind of computer class you would teach? I don't even know how to do email. So I don't know much about computers. But, we have had classes before with some success."

"I'd like to teach the UNIX operating system," answered Gerry.

"Well, we have Microsoft computers here. Is that the same as UNIX?"

Gerry threw up his arms in disgust, stood up and headed for the door.

"Damn stupid Windows! Forget I ever brought it up," he yelled.

~~~

Sasha Brown sat in the front room of the Carbon home with a warm cup of herbal tea in her hands. Elyse Carbon faced her in her chair by the picture window. Both of them had been thinking about Colt but were not able to get together until now. After reliving Colt's out-of-body experience and their part in his regaining consciousness, they turned to the latest news in Colt's life.

"So did you feel anything when he had the last thing happen to him? I heard that he almost died," asked Sasha.

"I feel so connected to that young man but I seem to have missed things lately. I was very surprised to hear what happened to him. I didn't feel a thing. Since then he has visited. So, I now have insight into what happened," said Elyse.

"What did happen to him?"

"He had a near-death event. He experienced dying and coming back. As he related the experience to me, it seemed to him like an extremely smart angel communicated with him."

"Oh, oh, that kind of event," said Sasha with a new understanding.

"There was no reason for me to be a part of that experience. He was taken care of. And, I think from now on he will need me less."

"But he's still so young and new to psychic abilities. Doesn't he still need guidance?"

"I had my own realization concerning that. He has grown up in the last year. And his future path will have a grounding affect on him. Marriage and a family can do that. My role was short and intense but it's mostly over now," Elyse replied.

"I guess even nice kids can end up having a family earlier than anybody expected," said Sasha.

"I have a feeling that it will all work out fine. That sweet girlfriend of his will make a great wife. She'll be good for Colt."

"I sure hope they're happy together." said Sasha

~~~

Fletcher Rowe sat in his dorm room which was almost empty. He and his friend John Freeman had just finished loading the computer equipment into a van. Fletcher was pleased that he was able to get his degree by mostly testing out of classes. But, it was never the primary goal while he attended Western. His passion was directed elsewhere. He became a legend on the Internet by doing impossible programming and hacking feats. But, after proving himself to other hackers and programmers, he wasn't sure what his next step would be.

Luckily he had listened to the one friend that worked for a real company.

"Man, you blew their minds at that last meeting. You had it all done in less than six months. Crap, they thought maybe you had a team of programmers and testers working with you," said John.

Fletcher was not impressed with himself. He still thought of minute snippets of code that could be improved and features that were not finished. He had a plan and had succeeded which to him was business as usual.

"Yeah, I thought they would like that I finished early. But I didn't think they would come through with the stock and the job. I guess I don't trust business guys," said Fletcher.

"So, can you change your lifestyle to work for a company? I know it's different," asked John.

"Uh, change? I talked to Malcolm about it. It sounded like he was going to let me do it my own way. He said he had other people to go to meetings and that stuff."

"Yeah, I guess that would be me. He must really like what you can bring to the table if you get that much freedom."

"Maybe he just figures I'd leave if I didn't like it. I think he wants to get more out of me for all that stock I got," smiled Fletcher.

~~~

Amy was sitting with Suzy in her small bedroom at home in Burien. She couldn't stop thinking about the life growing inside her and the upcoming wedding. She felt like she had somehow cheated fate's timeline and was victorious. No other outcome could have made her happier. Suzy was again jealous of her friend after initially thinking that Amy's situation was a big mess.

After seeing how happy Colt and Amy were, she now wished she had what Amy had.

"Okay, so I'm ready to help with all of this stuff coming up. I can see you will need somebody to take care of you. Wedding arrangements, baby showers. It will be like a tornado hitting you," said Suzy.

Amy hugged her friend. She was overcome with joy that her best friend would be with her on the journey of her life. It was the perfect topping on her big cake of happiness.

"Oh, it will be so much fun. I know it seems like a lot of stuff to deal with, but I don't even care. I'm just so happy," said Amy.

"You know, I thought this would be a nightmare, but now I've changed my mind. This is what you wanted all along. It just happened earlier than we expected."

"It turns out that even our parents aren't that upset about it. My mother can't wait to be a grandmother. Colt's father was a little mad but his mother told him to get used to the idea of Colt being a father and being married. After that Colt said that he eased up."

"At least I have a boyfriend now. I never thought that Bobby Jones and I would be an item but so far so good. He's a different guy since the rehab thing. It's like he has grabbed on to life."

"Maybe you'll be in the same spot I'm in soon," said Amy.

Suzy put up both arms with the palms of her hands facing her friend. Her head shook sideways like a bobble head doll.

"Let's not go overboard girl. I don't need to hear crazy talk. We're just dating. I'm not in any hurry to get married and have babies. I'm not even ready to think about it."

Amy looked at Suzy and smiled. She couldn't resist giving her another hug.

~~~

Colt and Bobby were in the Burien Starbucks drinking tall cups of coffee. School had just ended. They had been talking about the previous year and both were remembering the highlights. Bobby thought about his struggles with alcohol, rehab and finally ending up in a solid relationship. He knew that without Colt's support he probably would be in much worse shape. Colt felt that after it was all over, he had gained something that he never knew existed. He felt that he had a purpose, that life had meaning.

"I don't get it. Most guys would be bummed out and you just keep smiling. I still can't believe you're getting married," said Bobby.

"I was always confident but now I feel really solid. After that near-death thing, I don't worry about the future. I feel like everything will work out," answered Colt.

"What about being a dad. That's a lot of responsibility. No way I'm ready for that. It's huge, man."

"Dude, I almost died. Even though I wasn't afraid when it was happening, I see how stuff can happen fast. I always thought Amy and I would be together. So what if it's a little earlier than we thought. No big deal to me."

"What about making a living? If you don't finish school it could be hard to get a good job." asked Bobby.

Colt thought about job opportunities and college. A sense of connectedness to his immediate and extended family welled up. He felt very fortunate to have good people looking out for him.

"A job won't be a problem. I already have about ten offers. I guess the certifications that I have, really do help with some companies. Also, Fletcher said he could get me in. But, I think the best might be for me to keep working for the university," said Colt.

"How can you do that?"

"Robert Snow said he would hire me if I had to quit school. He said that there were a lot of options if I stayed. Maybe I can even finish my degree if I organize things right. I just feel that there are a lot of possibilities. So, this summer I'm looking into all of this stuff. Mr. Carbon is helping me too."

"Well, I guess it's all good then," said Bobby.

"Dude, it's all really, really good."

About The Author

George Matthew Cole lives in Burien, Washington with his wife and dog. After a long career in the computer support field, he became interested in writing after attending a creative writing class at a local community college. His first novel "Colt O'Brien Sees The Light" was published in 2009. "Colt O'Brien Grows Up" is the sequel.

Find more information about George Matthew Cole at his web site.

www.georgemcole.com

Also by George Matthew Cole

Colt O'Brien Sees The Light
El Porto Summer